許皓 Wesley 、浩爾 Howard ——— 著

English for

貿協商英講師
許皓 Wesley

專業口譯員
浩爾 Howard

Success

創譯兄弟
商英職人養成術

52週 英文質感 優雅升級

☑ 一週一篇，適當的分量、實用的內容
☑ 固定學習週計劃，事半功倍
☑ 兼顧商業口語能力與商業知識

Contents 目次

Season 1 Conversations / Socializing 對話社交

Season 2　Meetings and Telephone Communication　會議與電話溝通

Season 3 Presentations and Interactions 簡報及互動

Season 4 Written Communication 書信溝通

序一

學好真商英～ 52 個主題，52 週的商英故事書

首先感謝聯經出版社和主編李芃小姐，以及著作夥伴 Dean Brownless、Howard Chien，以及插畫家 Erigue Chong 的協力。

早期從事 HR 人資面試官，亦擔任十多年的升學以及商英企訓講師，在商英教學經歷中，曾任教於台商，日商，美商，與知名的阿里巴巴。這些年來，看過無數履歷，也解答許多商英問題；如 review 大家常知動詞用法（V. 複習），而大家在一些資料所看到的卻是更應知之商務名詞用法（N. 評論）；restaurant review 餐廳評論，自然不能稱作餐廳複習。(笑) 所以商英應是用一種 [真實情境] 應用的學習方式，會是您在選擇單純單字片語背誦前後應可先反覆閱讀的。

此書討論確立出 52 週，週記式的情境學習，以其中的情境故事力，相信非常適合學習語言的各類人士。其中的「商英譯起來」，更是集合多年經驗，將其中 [商務單字] 和 [商英會話高頻片語] 做分析，並從沿革中連結記憶，將之成為每篇簡單易懂的真實商英會話懶人包。

本書從一開始的初來乍到，學習入門的菜鳥到慢慢協助公司做各式商業活動；從辦公室對話到請假，加班，議價，會議談判，客戶管理，召開懲處，設立目標……等。

相信此書集合了你我辛勤上班的 52 週小故事，期許不只是語文工具書，更是一本實用有趣的商英故事書。

創譯兄弟

許皓 Wesley

序二

商用英文是專業，也是日常

對你來說，商務英文很遙遠嗎？

對我來說，商用英文不是以考試成績界定，而是日常溝通的延伸，以實戰論英雄。這本書，就是給讀者增進「日常感」的實戰大補帖。

我們對「商英」的想像，往往不脫「正式」、「高級」、「困難」、「有一定格式」。也因此，大家常常在商用書信選用比較「難」，比較「正式」的高級單字，此舉卻忽略了很大的關鍵因素：「文化」與「關係」。

歸根究柢，我們潛意識裡還是關注使用商用英文的「任務」，而忽略了「過程」。任務固然重要，但過程中培養的關係，甚至締結的友誼，其實更加深遠。

試想，一位講話「正式」，常使用「高級」「困難」成語的 A 同事，以及說話幽默風趣，性格友善親和的 B 同事，哪一位感覺比較容易相處來往呢？我們不妨反思一下，英文學了這麼久，是否會用英文交朋友，還是只會寫制式信件。

除了「用英文建立關係」這項關鍵能力，商用英文的溝通對象大多來自與我們相異的文化背景。以歐美文化為例，往往會先 small talk 再切入正題，而我們最不擅長的就是用英文閒聊！

這本書結合豐富情境、單字記憶補充、專業翻譯和插圖，期望給讀者最佳閱讀體驗和學習收穫。

筆者主要負責本書的英翻中，分享翻譯時的特別策略：有別於平時習慣的「生動派」跳脫字面直搗句意，筆者因應本書的學習性質，為方便學習者參照雙語，盡量採取不改動語序的「順譯」方式，且在翻出英文詞語意義的同時，刻意貼近英文字面，以利讀者回推理解，期發揮最佳輔助學習功效。

這本書能誕生，要感謝李芃主編的耐心。感謝 Wesley 老哥的專業精闢解析，讓讀者好學習好記憶。感謝我的愛爾蘭兄弟 Dean，創造出生動實用的情境內容。感謝插畫家 Erique 精緻的繪圖和用心，讓視覺呈現更加生動活潑。也謝謝閱讀至此的您，謝謝您選擇拿起這本書，相信不會讓您失望的。

創譯兄弟
浩爾 Howard

序三

As an English teacher for the last five years, I have been asked the same question time after time; "Teacher, how can I improve my conversational English to better understand native English speakers"? My answer has always been the same; speak like one of them! The desire for my students to seamlessly blend into English conversations was evident. How exactly could they achieve that, though? It was then that the idea for this book was born. I had to create something to provide for my students and others. I wanted to give them something that they could take with them into a multitude of situations and feel confident in their ability to converse and perform.

過去五年擔任英語教師，再三面對學生同樣的疑問：「老師，我要怎麼加強英文對話能力，來增進對英文母語人士的理解力呢？」我的答案始終如一。學他們說話！我的學生如此渴望融入英文會話的世界，昭然若揭。但究竟要怎麼達成呢？正值此時，本書的企劃靈感於焉誕生。我要為學生和其他朋友創造內容。我想給他們一份禮物，讓他們能夠應用於各類場合，自信對話，自信表現。

A large portion of this book is loosely based on my past experience and situations I have personally been involved in. Meeting and dealing with people in different situations gave me the inspiration to write this book. I have always been fascinated by people, human behavior, and interaction. I believe I can mold myself into any conversation, no matter the topic, social class, or environment, and I know many people don't have that skill. However, it can be learnt.

本書大多篇幅來自我的過往經驗和曾經親身經歷的現場。各場合的人際交流，化為書寫靈感。素來，我著迷於「人」的行為與互動。我自信能夠融入任何對話，無論主題、社會階級，或環境為何；我知道，許多人沒有這樣的技能。不過，這技能是學得來的。

Combining my knowledge and experience I created 52 different units based on daily interactions focusing on work and entertainment settings. Learn how to flawlessly deal with different people and gain a better understanding of common idioms, slang and behavioural cues.

結合我的知識與經驗，我打造出 52 個單元內容，聚焦工作與休閒生活場景。一起來學習順暢溝通，熟悉常用俚語諺語，並領略人際互動的秘訣。

By reading and studying the units you will be well able to communicate with English speakers on a global scale. In this busy age of information sharing, we can sometimes forget and lose a lot of what is valuable. There is no greater feeling than providing valuable information to people that they can use in their daily lives. Whether you're a college student, graduate, or business professional, this book is for you!

Regardless of how you use it, I truly believe this book will help you take your English communication and understanding to the next level.

閱讀、學習本書各單元的你，將能夠與世界舞台的英文人士妥善溝通。現今繁忙的資訊共享時代，我們不免遺忘、丟失珍貴的事物。我想，提供珍貴資訊給大眾，讓其得以運用在日常生活中，應該是世界上最棒的感覺了。無論你是大學生、畢業生，或者商務專業人士，這本書正是為你而寫！不論你怎麼使用本書，我真切相信，這本書會助你升級英文溝通和理解力，來到更高境界。

Dean Brownless

浩爾 Howard
許皓 Wesley

Dean Brownless

Season 1

Conversations / Socializing

對話社交

The Handshake
握手透露的秘密

"Oh, his hand was super sweaty and his handshake was so weak… so…I'm not sure if we should hire him. "

「喔，他的手汗好多，而且握起手來軟綿綿沒力氣……我不太確定該不該錄取他。」

Squeeze too tightly and you **come across as power hungry**, **domineering** and appear to have evil plans to take over the world. If your grip is not firm enough (like you've just caught a wet fish) then you're perceived as weak and untrustworthy. The importance of a firm handshake can never be underestimated. In Eastern cultures the handshake is seen as an unnecessary form of contact. A way to spread germs and an overall awkward manner. It is encouraged for business purposes, particularly in the Western world, however, it may not always be executed effectively.

手握太緊**讓人感覺過度渴望權力**，**控制欲強**，好像盤算著統治世界的邪惡計畫。若握得有氣無力（感覺好像握不住剛撈起的魚），則給人有虛弱且不值得信任的印象。握手是否有力，重要性不可小覷。東方文化中，握手不是必要的交際禮儀，而且可能因此傳播病菌，或被認為很彆扭。尤其是西方文化，特別鼓勵在商業場合握手交誼。然而，握手之道不是人人都能掌握。

Typically, people of higher position or authority should **initiate** the handshake. For example, in an interview setting; the interviewer will naturally lead the meeting. The same can be said if you are **meeting the in-laws**. For circumstances in which the person of higher authority does not offer their hand, then you **are within your rights** to offer yours and initiate the handshake. Don't be shy!

通常，位階較高的人會**主動**握手。例如在面試場合，面試官會自然地主導面試。同樣的，你在**跟另一半的父母見面時**，長輩會主動表示。若長輩未主動伸出手，你**可以**主動握手。別害羞！

The **general consensus** is that a weak handshake portrays a weak character. This is of course a generalisation, although, you would be surprised at how many people judge you based on your handshake. Obviously, if someone has a medical condition then they can be forgiven in this situation for offering a limp hand. **On the flip side**, a firm handshake conveys strength and confidence in said person and their abilities. We may not always be confident inside but let's **get off on the right foot** at least on the outside.

一般認為握手軟弱無力代表性格軟弱。當然，這是種概括化的看法。不過，如果知道有多少人會以握手來判斷人，你可能會感到很訝異。顯然，如果是生病的關係而握手無力，那情有可原。**相反地**，握手堅實有力則是展示了力量、自信與能力。儘管我們未必永遠自信滿滿，但讓我們可以**先讓**行為**看起來有自信**！

The significance of a firm handshake must not be overstated. In the next unit we will examine the key points to remember when shaking hands and how to ace that awkward encounter.

握手厚實有力，再強調也不為過。接下來，我們會一一審視握手時的重點，並且告訴你怎麼扭轉尷尬的窘境。

商英譯起來

come across as ...

"come across as + 名詞／形容詞"，主詞為人時，意思為「給人……印象」。若主詞為事物則表示「事物表達出……」的意思。"come across..." 則表示「遇到某人」或「不經意發現某事物」。

power hungry

(a.) 表示對權力非常渴望。

domineering

(a.) 為形容詞，表示控制慾強的。

initiate

(v.) 表示開始；發動；主動的意思。

meeting the in-laws

In-law 為姻親的意思。岳父、公公為 "father-in-law"，岳母、婆婆則為 "mother-in-law"，所以 "meeting the in-laws" 在此是指與對象的長輩或親戚見面。

are within your rights

"be within one's rights to do something" 是指「某人去做某事是正當的」。

general consensus

一般認知，普遍共識。

on the flip side

反過來說；意義相當於 "on the contrary"。 "on the other hand" 則是「另一方面來說」的意思。

get off on the right foot

有一個好的開始，特別是指在 (工作任務或關係上)。

Week 02

The Handshake
從握手看人

Following an interview meeting; Howard (H) and Wesley (W) discuss Dave's (D) chances of getting the job.

面試結束後，浩爾和衛斯理討論著戴夫錄取的機會有多大。

Wesley： Well..? What'd you think of Dave? He didn't get off on the right foot with a handshake like that did he? I mean, his hand was weak and limp. I wasn't sure if he was alive or not.

衛斯理： 嗯……你覺得戴夫怎麼樣？他從一開始的握手就沒有好的開始，對吧？我是說，他的手感覺軟弱無力，都不知道他是不是活著的。

Howard： Actually, I think he has a lot of experience and he could be **a great asset to our team** even though he's been **between jobs** for quite a while now.

浩爾： 其實，我覺得他經驗相當豐富，可以為我們團隊**增色不少**，雖然他已經**待業**了好一陣子。

Wesley： I don't, Howard. I usually am **a good judge of character** and when someone shakes my hand like that, I usually don't trust them in some way. I'm just not sure about him.

衛斯理： 我不認為耶，浩爾。通常我**看人頗準**。握手虛弱無力的人，我通常不完全信任。就是感覺他怪怪的。

Howard： Is this your **gut feeling** that's telling you this? I felt like his first impression wasn't too bad.

浩爾： 是你的**直覺**判斷嗎？我覺得他給人的第一印象不算太糟。

Wesley： Maybe I'm overreacting but you know what I always say, **you never get a second chance to make a first impression.**

衛斯理： 也許是我反應過度，但你也知道，我常說：「**第一印象的機會，錯過就不再有。**」

Howard： That's true, however, on the flip side he does have excellent problem-solving skills and he will bring **a breath of fresh air** into our department. So, I am going to **make the call** on this one and hire Dave. I will have Mary in HR do the necessary paperwork.

浩爾： 的確。不過，反過來說，他真的具備優秀的問題解決能力，能為我們部門帶來**新氣象**。所以我就**決定**錄取戴夫！我會再請人資的瑪麗處理文書作業。

Wesley： Okay, that's fine but don't come crying to me in 6 month's time when he **screws us over.**

衛斯理： 好吧，就這樣吧，但若半年後他**搞砸**了，你不要哭著跑來找我。

Howard： Trust me on this one, I **got your back**!

浩爾： 相信我吧，**有我頂著！**

ABC 商英譯起來

a great asset to the team
asset (n.) 優點、長處、有用的人；"a great asset to the team" 通常指團隊中有重大貢獻的得力助手、主將。

between jobs
是「失業」"unemployed" 的委婉說法，字面上就是介於上一個和下一個即將到來的工作的意思，就是 "between jobs"「待業中」。

a good judge of character
judge (n.) 鑒定人；鑒賞家。"a good / bad judge of character" 意指「善於 / 不善於看人」。

gut feeling
直覺，本能的感覺。

you never get a second chance to make a first impression
第一印象沒有機會重頭來過。

a breath of fresh air
就像一陣清新的空氣。（形容令人耳目一新帶來了新氣象）

make the call
call (n.) 在這裡為「決定」的意思，"make the call" 則表做決定。

screws us over
screw 當動詞為旋轉、旋緊（螺絲），而 "scre sb over" 則有讓人或事情搞砸之意。"screw up" 也有搞砸的意思。

got one's back
或 "have (got) one's back" 表支持且會積極幫助某人。也用來表示當同事或朋友間需要協助時，會力挺。

Small Talk
閒聊哈啦

Dave has recently started his new job and is **learning the ropes** from his new colleagues Sarah and Dean.

戴夫最近開始了新工作，並跟新同事莎拉、迪恩**學習新工作的流程及方法**。

Dean： Sarah, this is Dave, he's the **new fish** here in the department. I hope you will make him feel welcome.

迪恩： 莎拉，這位是戴夫。他是我們部門的**新人**。希望妳好好歡迎他啊。

Sarah and Dave shake hands
（莎拉和戴夫握手）

Sarah： Hi Dave, very nice to meet you. When did you start?

莎拉： 嗨，戴夫，幸會。你什麼時候開始上班的？

Dave： I just started yesterday yeah, I'm still **finding my feet**. Don't really know too many people.

戴夫： 昨天剛開始，我還**在摸索中**。也還不太認識大家。

Dean： **Good stuff,** welcome aboard anyway. How did you **fare** after the typhoon yesterday? Was your place damaged?

迪恩： 做得好。歡迎加入！昨天颱風，一切**都還好嗎**？家裡有沒有怎麼樣？

- -

Dave： No, thankfully all was fine. We **battened down the hatches**. It was a little **hairy** at times.

戴夫： 沒事，謝天謝地一切都好。我們**做了充足準備**。中間幾度情況有點**驚險**。

Sarah： You were well prepared! My bedroom window was smashed and there was glass everywhere. I was a little **shook up**.

莎拉： 你已做了萬全準備！我家臥室窗戶破了，玻璃碎滿地。我**嚇了一跳**。

Dave： That's scary. I'm terrified of earthquakes because we just don't get them in my **neck of the woods.**

戴夫： 真恐怖。我很怕地震，因為**老家**完全沒這東西。

Dean： Well, at least you are both fine. Sarah, let's pop down and show Dave the cafeteria and our other facilities. We've got **safety in numbers** which means Ian in Accounts won't bother me about next month's target.

迪恩： 嗯，至少你們兩個都沒事。莎拉，我們帶戴夫下樓看看餐廳和其他設施。我們**人多勢眾**，會計部的伊恩比較不會來煩我要下個月的業績。

All three co-workers leave the working area...en route to the cafeteria...
（三位同事離開辦公區，前往餐廳）

Sarah： So Dave, how was your weekend? What do you like to do in your **downtime**?

莎拉： 戴夫，**週末**過得如何？你平時的休閒活動是什麼？

Dave： Yeah, I love to do yoga when I don't have my hands full with the kids.

戴夫： 不用忙孩子時，我喜歡做瑜珈。

Sarah： **Tell me about it!**

莎拉： **我完全懂！**

ABC 商英譯起來

learning the ropes

"learn the ropes" 此一片語，來自水手用語，初上船的水手必須學習綁船桅的繩結，後來便引申為「學習做某事的準則及方法」。也可以說某人 "know the ropes"，表示「知道某事的訣竅」。

new fish

俚語，新人、菜鳥的意思。

finding my feet

"find my feet" 有「熟悉並開始能掌握」之意。

good stuff

"good stuff / great stuff" 都是用來鼓勵別人做得好的意思。

how did you fare?

經過某件事情，詢問對方後續或狀況是否依然安好。這裡的 "fare" 相當於 do 的意思，如："How did you fare(=do) on your math exam?"

battened down the hatches

batten (v.) 釘住、封住；hatch (n.) 船艙口。"batten down the hatches" 原指在風暴來臨前將船的艙門封住、釘牢之意，後來引申為做好準備，預防不好的狀況發生，也就是「防範未然」的意思。

hairy

口語用法，為「驚險」的意思。通常是沒有生命危險，只是驚險，帶有一點刺激的感覺。

shook up

"shake sb up" 指令人感到震驚或是被震撼到的意思。

my neck of the woods

"one's neck of woods" 某人的居住地或老家附近一帶的地區。

safety in numbers

經由數量就產生安全感，也就是一般所指的人多勢眾。常用 "There's safety in numbers."。

downtime

不用上班或休閒的時候。

tell me about it

還用你說；可不是嗎，在感同身受，了解對方感受時可說的話。

Week 04

Small Talk
辦公室裡的閒扯二三事

Wesley is chatting with Neil from IT but it appears Neil is **out of his depth.**

衛斯理和 IT 部門的尼爾正在聊天，但尼爾好像**搭不上話**。

Wesley： So Neil, how's everything with you, any news?

衛斯理： 尼爾，最近都還好嗎？有什麼新消息？

Neil： Uhh, nothing special.

尼爾： 呃……沒什麼特別的。

Wesley： Oh ok. How's work going these days now that we are nearing the end of the financial year?

衛斯理： 喔，好喔。快要年底作帳了，最近工作如何？

Neil： Busy.

尼爾： 蠻忙的。

Wesley： Oh I see. I'm the same. Listen, Neil, I wanted to **get your take on** some laptop recommendations. I'm going to treat **the missus** for her birthday next week so I'm hoping you can **come up with the goods** for me!?

衛斯理： 了解。我也是。嘿，尼爾，我想聽聽**你**有沒有推薦的筆電，我要送**老婆**大人當她下禮拜的生日禮物，你能不能幫我找台超讚的電腦？

Neil： It depends on your salary and how much you want to spend. How much do you make a month?

尼爾： 要看你薪水，還有願意花多少。你一個月賺多少錢？

Wesley： Why does that matter? I just want something nice for my wife and don't want **to break the bank**.

衛斯理： 跟薪水有什麼關係？我只是想買個好禮物給太太，而且不用**荷包大失血**。

Neil： The new Asus Terminator XT9001 is a beast.

尼爾： 華碩新的 Terminator XT9001 很猛。

***Neil abruptly finishes the conversation by walking away. ***
（尼爾突然走掉，結束對話。）

***Wesley returns to his work space a little **taken aback** by his recent conversation with Neil and bumps into Sarah along the way. ***
（衛斯理走回自己位置，對於尼爾的突兀感到有點**錯愕**，剛好遇到莎拉。）

Wesley： Hey, I just spoke with Neil outside the conference area and I pretty much did all the talking. The only thing he asked me about was my salary which I thought was a little rude. I mean, it's none of his business how much money I make anyway. Can you believe that guy?

衛斯理： 嘿，我剛才在會議室外面跟尼爾聊天，幾乎都是我在講話。他唯一問我的是我薪水多少，蠻沒禮貌的。我是說，我賺多少反正不關他的事啊。他竟然這樣問，很扯吧！

Sarah： Who's that Neil, from IT? Oh yeah, talking to him is like trying to **get blood from a stone**. I'll catch you later I'm meeting a client down in the lobby.

莎拉： 尼爾，誰啊？ IT 那個嗎？喔對啊，跟他講話根本就是**自找麻煩**。待會再跟你聊，我先下去大廳跟客戶開個會。

商英譯起來

out of his depth

depth 指水的深度。"out of one's depth" 意指超過某人理解範圍，對某人來說是困難的。

your take on...

"one's take on..."，「某人對於……的看法」。"Your take on..." 也就是「你對於……的看法」。

the missus

就是 Mrs.，亦同 wife，是比較口語化的稱呼，帶有我太太、內人或老婆大人的意味。

come up with the goods

達到要求，不負期待的意思。也可以用 "deliver the goods"。

break the bank

這裡的 bank 指的是家裡的老本或是小豬撲滿，把老本都拿出來全砸了或是砸破小豬撲滿，即代表著要花大錢啦！

taken aback

錯愕，讓人反應不過來，吃了一驚。"take sb aback" 就是讓某人大吃一驚的意思。

get blood from a stone

指不論多麼用力請求，要讓某人幫忙難如登天。

Week 05

Asking for help
拜託！

Dave **confides in** Howard for some much needed help as he aims to learn more about the company's operating system.

戴夫想學會公司的作業系統，於是**私下**向浩爾**發出**求助訊號。

Dave：　Hey Howard, how are you? Can I **pick your brain** for a second?

戴夫：　嘿，浩爾，你好嗎？可不可以**跟你請教**一下？

Howard：　Yeah sure what's up?

浩爾：　喔，好啊，怎麼啦？

Dave：　The thing is, I'm really struggling to **get to grips** with this new operating system that we have. Do you think you could go over it with me if you get a chance?

戴夫： 是這樣的，我很努力要**學會並操作**這套新的作業系統。可以的話，能請你教我操作一遍嗎？

Howard： Sure, no worries at all. Do you have time later on after lunch? It will take around about two hours to show you **the ins and outs** of that system because it's currently running on our individual Blockchain system so if you are unfamiliar with that; it can be **daunting**.

浩爾： 好啊，完全沒問題。等一下午餐後你有空嗎？我可以示範這個系統的**操作細節**，大概要兩個小時。因為系統是建構在我們的獨立區塊鏈上，如果你不熟區塊鏈，可能會**覺得很難**。

Dave： Ah brilliant, I have a basic understanding but **a refresher** would be much appreciated.

戴夫： 啊，太棒了。我有基礎概念，但如果你能幫我**複習一下**，那就太感激了。

Howard： Perfect! Let's **set aside** 2-4pm in meeting room 7?

浩爾： 完美！我們就**安排**下午 2 點到 4 點，7 號會議室見囉？

Dave： Sorted! Thanks again. **I owe you one!**

戴夫： 搞定！謝謝啦。**欠你一次！**

Howard： Don't thank me just yet, ha-ha.

浩爾： 學完再謝我吧，哈哈！

🔤 商英譯起來

confind in

"confined in sb"，私下向某人傾訴秘密。

pick your brain

字面上有從別人的腦子裡挑東西，引申為「討教、請教」之意。

get to grips

grip (n.) 握緊、抓住。"get to grips" 指開始了解並能著手處理事件的意思。

the ins and outs

要做好某事或工作所需具備的細節。

daunting

形容任務或工作的難度令人卻步或是生畏。

a refresher

喚起某人對某事的記憶或提醒之意。

set aside

為了完成重要的事情，特地敲定並且撥空出來。

I owe you one

欠你一次，代表對方幫你解決了一個棘手的問題，在心裡惦記著這份人情。

Politely declining an offer to a company dinner

禮貌性婉拒公司的晚餐派對

Howard, Wesley and Dean invite new candidate Dave to a dinner and drinks party with the rest of the staff from the company.

浩爾、衛斯理和迪恩邀請新人戴夫一起參加公司同事的晚餐派對。

Dean： Dave, it's been a minute! I **haven't seen you in forever**. We're all heading out for dinner and drinks. Are you **keen**?

迪恩： 戴夫，一分鐘不見，**就覺得過了好久**！我們要出發去晚餐派對了。你**想要**一起來嗎？

Howard： Yeah, you should come Dave. It's a **last-minute** thing but it'll be fun. Come on, **let your hair down**! It looks like you've been **burning the candle at both ends** recently.

浩爾： 對啊，戴夫，你應該一起來。雖然**現在才約**，但一定很好玩。來吧，**輕鬆一下**！感覺你最近都**操勞過度**。

Dave： I wish I'd known sooner but I have to finish this project for my new clients in New Delhi and Singapore. I haven't got a clue what they were thinking when they placed this order but I have **to get my head around** it. The last thing I want is **to be in the firing line** right now. I don't need that.

戴夫： 真希望早點知道要聚餐，可是我得先幫我新德里和

新加坡的新客戶把案子完成。我還不太清楚當初他們下單時候的想法，但我一定要**搞懂**才行。畢竟我最不想發生的事就是**被叮得滿頭包**，我不需要。

Wesley： Come on. You deserve **to let your hair down** every once in a while. We all do.

衛斯理： 拜託，你應該偶爾**放鬆**一下，我們都需要。

Dave： Thanks for the kind invitation guys but definitely next time. My schedule will be a lot lighter at the end of this month. We could all go and catch that new America Captain sequel?

戴夫： 謝謝你們熱情地邀我，但真的要下次了。我月底行程比較不忙。到時我們再一起去看《隊長美國》續集，好嗎？

Wesley： You mean Captain America? Yeah **I'm down for** that at the end of the month. Anyway, listen, we'd better **make tracks**. We have an 8pm reservation at that **swanky** steakhouse down on Forest Avenue and traffic is getting **sticky** as we speak. **Adios** Dave, take care.

衛斯理： 你是說《美國隊長》吧？好啊，月底我**可以**！好吧，我們**得走了**。我們訂的餐廳是森林大道一家很**時尚**的牛排館，8 點的訂位。路上越來越塞了。 **掰啦，**

戴夫，加油。

Dave： Thanks again guys, enjoy your evening. Have a beer for me won't you?

戴夫： 謝啦。玩得開心。幫我多喝一杯啤酒啦。

- -

Dean & Howard： Oh don't worry we will.

迪恩＆浩爾： 放心，一定。

Wesley： Maybe even two!

衛斯理： 可能多喝兩杯吧！

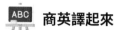 **商英譯起來**

I haven't seen you in forever

好久沒有見到你，久到簡直恍如隔世了！"in forever"也可以用"for ages"代換。通常不會單獨使用，後面會再加一個問候，或是接著討論想要講的事情。

keen

(a.) 渴望的，"be keen to …"指「渴望，熱衷去做……」。

last-minute

最後一刻的，指的是某事完成前的最後關頭。

let your hair down

要睡覺了放鬆時會把頭髮放下來，這句就是放輕鬆的意思。

burning the candle at both ends

"burn the candle at both ends" 字面為蠟燭兩頭燒的意思，引申為「過度勞累」。

get my head around it

[英式] 理解，搞懂，同 understand。

in the firing line

指的是「親上火線」或「受到責備或批評的第一線」。

I'm down for...

附和前面的人的意見，表示自己也想要參與其中！

make tracks

該快速離開現在所在地了。

swanky

(a.) 時髦而奢華的。

sticky

(a.) 本為黏稠之意，這裡說交通會黏稠，也就代表著車多流量，人多的意思。

Adios

此為西班牙語中的「再會」 ，現在也普及化用於英語系國家中代表熱情的道再見，good-bye。

Week 07

Work Dinner
尾牙

Dean, Howard, Wesley and the rest of the staff are out for dinner and drinks to celebrate a successful year.

迪恩、浩爾、衛斯理和同事聚餐，喝小酒，慶祝成功的一年。

Howard： It's refreshing to get the **recognition** from our senior managers after a busy year. I think we all deserve a **decent** raise or big bonus to justify all the **blood, sweat and tears** we **put into** the business. What do you think guys?

浩爾： 忙完一年得到長官**嘉許**真不錯。我認為我們都值得一份**像樣的**加薪或分紅，才對得起所有**投入的精力及心血**。你們覺得呢？

Wesley： Let's not **talk shop** while we are trying to enjoy ourselves?!

衛斯理： 不要再**聊工作**啦！派對就是要好好玩啊！

Dean： Yeah, good idea let's **put that on the back burner** for now and just enjoy the evening. Let's get through tonight and see how we go. I mean, we still have Christmas and Chinese New Year to **tackle**.

迪恩： 對啊，好主意，加薪的事**之後再說**，現在就好好玩吧。過完今晚再看接下來如何。我們還有聖誕和中國新年要**過**呢。

Howard： **Fair point**, I agree.

浩爾： **有道理**，我同意。

Wesley： It looks like everyone knows what they want to order. What do we want to have? You guys are okay with sharing yeah?

衛斯理： 大家好像都決定要點什麼了。我們要點什麼？大家
一起吃，你們不介意吧？

Dean & Howard： Sure, of course.

迪恩 & 浩爾： 當然沒關係啊。

Dean： What drinks are we going **to order for the table**? Beer or wine?

迪恩： **這桌要點什麼喝的**？啤酒或紅白酒？

Howard： Both!

浩爾： 都要！

Wesley： I take it we're **going all out** tonight!

衛斯理： 看來今晚大家都**豁出去**了喔！

Howard： Stick it **on the tab**, who cares anyway. We deserve it.

浩爾： 都**記到帳上**，管他的。我們應得的。

Dean： By tab do you mean company credit card ha-ha?

迪恩： 帳上，你是說公司的信用卡嗎哈哈？

Wesley： Same same, right?

衛斯理： 都差不多啦，是吧？

📇 商英譯起來

recognition
嘉許，讚賞，表揚。

decent
(a.) 像樣的，相當不錯的，質感很優的。

blood, sweat and tears
血水、汗水以及淚水的交織，形容非常辛苦的過程。

put into
投入、花費大量（精力、時間）的意思。比如 "put into a lot of efforts / energy" 都是常見的用法。

talk shop
在辦公室以外的地方談論工作。

put that on the back burner
暫時擱置一旁，之後再說。美國的廚房裡，爐台上一般都有四個電爐口，前後各兩個，人們會把一些要慢慢煮的食物放在後面的兩個爐口上。用來指事情不緊急可以擱置的意思。

tackle
(v.) 處理、對付的意思。

fair point
說得很正確，很有道理。

order for the table

這裡的 table 指的是餐桌，也就是說，這一桌要點什麼呢？

going all out

"go all out"意指豁出去了，鼓足幹勁。

on the tab

在國外酒吧的文化裡，當地人大多習慣用信用卡或現金卡付帳。他們會把卡片交給 bartender 說 "Keep it open."代表先收信用卡之後再結帳。然後開始點就會說 "Put it on my tab"，意思是放在我的帳上。看到別人或同伴點的食物或飲料，也想點相同的東西，就會在對方點完後跟服務生說 "Make it two."，也就是「我也要一樣的」。

Entertaining Foreign Clients
款待外國客戶

Kate, Howard and Wesley have been set the task of entertaining their foreign customers whilst they are in town. They decide to eat at a local restaurant to give their customers a feel for the city. Their customers are Brad (USA), Stephen (Ireland) , Prandeepi (India) and Lewis (Hong Kong).

凱特、浩爾和衛斯理獲派接待外國客戶，當客戶來訪時，他們決定帶客戶到當地的餐廳，體驗這城市的文化。他們的客戶為來自美國的布萊德、愛爾蘭的史蒂芬、印度的龐迪皮，還有香港的路易斯。

Kate： It's great to finally meet you all having been in close communication for the last year and a half. It feels like we all **go way back** ha-ha. Are you all **keen** to try some local **delicacies**?

凱特： 我們密切聯絡了一年半，終於見面了，真開心。感覺好像**認識好久好久**，呵呵。你們**期待**台灣當地的**美食**嗎？

All four customers： Sure, why not!

客戶： 當然啊！

Howard： Yeah I think these dishes are **not to be missed**.

浩爾： 我們**不能錯過**這些菜。

Lewis： I may have tried some of them before but I'm happy for you all to recommend your favourites.

路易斯： 有一些我可能吃過了，但你們推薦自己最愛的菜吧，我想知道。

Brad： I think I'm happy to try anything. I consider myself the adventurous type.

布萊德： 我都想試試看。我是比較勇於嚐鮮的人。

Prandeepi & Stephen： We're just **ravenous**!

龐迪皮＆史蒂芬： 我們**餓昏了**！

Stephen： All I had was some Oolong tea and a banana at that meeting earlier. So, I could **eat a horse**!

史蒂芬： 剛剛開會我只喝了點烏龍茶，吃了香蕉。我現在**餓到吃得下一匹馬**。

Wesley： Unfortunately, horse isn't on the menu but we do have some other treats for you all ha-ha.

衛斯理： 可惜菜單上沒有馬，但有其他好吃的可以介紹給你們，哈哈。

*** Food arrives at the table***
（上菜）

Prandeepi： Wow this all looks incredible. What is this **concoction**?

龐迪普： 哇，看起來好讚。這一桌是什麼**組合的菜餚**？

Howard： Well, we ordered a mix of food to **start** our evening **off on the right foot**. Here we have scallion crepes, pork chop rice, beef noodle soup, steamed dumplings, pigs blood cake and pot stickers.

浩爾： 嗯，我們點了不同種類的菜，來**展開**美好的夜晚。有蔥油餅、豬排飯、牛肉湯麵、小籠包、豬血糕，還有鍋貼。

Brad： And what's this here?

布萊德： 這道是什麼？

Kate： I think that's chicken heart and this here is cow tongue soup. Would you guys like to try this first?

凱特： 那個是雞心，這碗是牛舌湯。你們要不要先試試看？

Stephen： I'm starving but I'm a little picky. I don't think I can eat the chicken heart or cow tongue soup. A lot of people **get bent out of shape** when I tell them I'm picky but I am just not used to this type of food, sorry.

史蒂芬： 我餓壞了，但我滿挑的。我可能吃不下雞心或牛舌湯。很多人聽到我這樣說就蠻**沮喪**的，但我真的不太習慣這類食物，抱歉。

Kate： No problem Stephen, I can understand. Why don't you try some of this scallion crepe and beef noodle soup to start. It's very delicious and I don't think it is too extreme for you.

凱特： 沒問題，史蒂芬，我了解。要不要試試看蔥油餅和牛肉湯麵？很好吃喔，你應該也可以接受。

Howard： Great! Let's **dig in**. You all know how to use chopsticks, right?

浩爾： 太好了！**開動**吧。你們都會用筷子吧？

商英譯起來

go way back

"go back"彼此認識很久的意思，也可以說"go back a long way"或"go way back"。

delicacies

(n.) "delicacy" 美食、佳餚。

not to be missed

絕不能錯過，錯過就會後悔的意思。

ravenous

(a.) 餓昏頭，飢餓的，跟 starving 是一樣的意思。

eat a horse

餓到可以吃掉一匹馬。比喻極度飢餓的狀態。

concoction

(n.) 拼湊、混合出來的東西。在這裡指上了各式各樣的菜。

start off on the right foot

踏出美好的第一步，出師告捷之急。

get bent out of shape

bent 是彎，"out of shape"是彎到扭曲不成形。彎的都不成樣了，就是非常生氣、沮喪的意思。

dig in

開動、開始吃的意思。

Week 09

Entertaining and Advising
給辦公室戀情的忠告

The group spends the rest of the night at the karaoke bar, however, not everyone has singing on their minds. While the rest of the group are singing and drinking alcohol; Brad and Wesley are in deep discussion.

一行人接下來的行程在 KTV 度過。但並不是所有人都想唱歌。當大家引吭高歌，大口喝酒的時候，布萊德和衛斯理正在認真討論事情。

Wesley： Cheers! Brad!

衛斯理： 布萊德！乾杯！

Brad： Cheers! Thanks for showing us the city this evening. It's great to get a local's perspective of the place.

布萊德： 乾杯！謝謝你們今晚帶著我們遊覽城市。有在地人導覽真好。

Wesley： No worries, anytime. Let's **crack open** this bottle of scotch and get the party started eh?

衛斯理： 別客氣。我們來**開這瓶**蘇格蘭威士忌，讓派對開始吧？

Brad： Why not? **When in Rome...**

布萊德： 好啊，**入境隨俗**。

Brad moves slightly closer to Wesley
（布萊德坐靠近衛斯理）

Brad： Listen Wesley, you know Kate? Ehhh, **is** she **spoken for** or does she have **a hubby**? I think she is gorgeous.

布萊德： 嘿，衛斯理，你認識凱特嗎？她**有對象**或是**結婚**了嗎？我覺得她很正。

Wesley： You're **preaching to the choir** man, I agree. But, you're **entering dangerous territory**.

衛斯理： 嘿，**我也覺得**。但是你這樣**很危險喔**。

Brad： Why? I thought bec-

布萊德： 為什麼？是因為……

Wesley interrupts Brad
（衛斯理打斷布萊德）

Wesley： Come on man, we all know from **office politics 101, you don't shit where you eat**.

衛斯理： 拜託，我們都知道**辦公室守則第一課：不談辦公室戀情**。

Brad： That's true but I don't work in her office.

布萊德： 是啦，但我又不跟她同辦公室。

Wesley： **Tread carefully**. That's all I can say.

衛斯理： 我只能說**小心為妙**。

Brad： I think I'll take my chances. It could be **the drink talking** but, I really feel something for her.

布萊德： 我還是會試試看。可能是**酒精作祟**，但我真的對她有感覺。

商英譯起來

crack open

"crack (open) …" 可指砸開、打開，在這裡指把酒打開。

when in Rome

整句話是 "When in Rome, do as the Romans do"，入境隨俗的意思。

is spoken for

"be spoken for" 有物品已有人訂購之意，如果用來表達人，則表示此人已名花有主，也可用 "She is seeing someone"，代表已有交往的對象。

hubby

husband 的口語用法。"husband and wife"，夫妻，也可說成 "hubby and wifey"，有俏皮親暱之意。

preaching to the choir

preach（v.），是傳教的意思，"preacher choir" 則是牧師。有合唱團或教堂唱詩班的意思。"preacheing to the choir" 對唱詩班傳教，簡直是多此一舉。這裡是表示「不用跟我說，我早就這麼想了！」

entering dangerous territory

territory（n.）通常用於地盤、領地，在這裡代表置於危險之中。

office politics 101, you don't shit where you eat

不在用餐的地方解手 = 不在常待的地方惹麻煩。後來也用來表示不跟同事談辦公室戀情。

tread carefully

tread (v.) 走路,"tread carefully" 有小心謹慎之意。

the drink talking

字面上翻過來的意思是,在講話的是酒精,不是自己本來想要說的話,也就是說由於酒精作祟,藉酒壯膽說出某些話。

Preparing for a business trip
準備出差

Dave and Howard are discussing their upcoming business trips in the office juice bar.

戴夫和浩爾在辦公室的飲料區討論最近要出差的行程。

Howard： **All systems go** for next week Dave?

浩爾： 下週出差**準備就緒了嗎**，戴夫？

Dave： I wish. I've been **having butterflies** all week. I guess it's because I'm taking my first business trip with **the gaffer**.

戴夫： 是就好了。我整個禮拜都**很緊張**。我猜是因為我第一次要跟**主管**出差吧。

Howard： Are you flying business class?

浩爾： 你們搭商務艙嗎？

Dave： Nah, I don't think so. I feel like this last year head office have started to **rein in our perks**, which kinda sucks. The good times are over, well not quite, but, you know what I mean.

戴夫： 沒有吧。我覺得今年上頭開始**限制我們的津貼**，滿討厭的。好日子結束了，雖是沒到很糟，但你懂我意思。

Howard： I'm **in the same boat** as you Dave.

浩爾： 我跟你在**同一艘船上**，戴夫。

Dave： What? No, I'm flying.

戴夫： 什麼？不是啊，我是要搭飛機去耶。

Howard： No, it's just an expression. I'm saying I will also have a business trip next week with my boss. It should be eventful as we don't really **see eye to eye**. I have to give a presentation to our clients in Manchester, England. He's coming to secure the deal and **put the foot down** as they've been **stalling** recently on our proposal. Just a **heads-up** Dave, have you applied for your visa **and all that**? Remember, you must have it granted before you go to India.

浩爾： 不是啦，只是一個說法。我是說我下禮拜也要跟老闆出差。應該會有一些狀況，畢竟我跟他的**想法不同**。我要對英國曼徹斯特的客戶簡報。老闆去是要確保案子會下來並**表明立場**，因為他們最近都把我們的提案**推遲**。戴夫，**提醒一下**，你辦好簽證那些了嗎？記得你出發去印度前要拿到喔。

Dave： Oh shoot, no! I haven't gotten the confirmation email yet. I better **make tracks**. **Gotta run, catch ya later**.

戴夫： 啊，糟糕，還沒！我還沒收到確認信。我得**先走了**。**先去忙了，待會聊**。

Howard： Break a leg!

浩爾： 祝你好運，一切順利！

Dave： Thanks, you too!

戴夫： 謝啦，你也是！

商英譯起來

all systems (are) go

go (n.) 進行，"all systems (are) go" 原本是用來指火箭升空發射前，系統準備就緒的意思。用在日常生活中，指一切都準備就緒，可以進行了。

having butterflies (in one's stomach)

胃裡在攪動，就像蝴蝶拍動翅膀，代表對即將要做的事感到很不安、緊張。

the gaffer

[英式] 領班、工頭，在這指「主管」的意思。

rein in our perks

"rein in" 為控制、限制的意思，"perk" 則是工作津貼、福利之意。也就是減少我們的津貼 / 福利。

in the same boat

表達在同一艘船上的同理心，也就是在同一陣線上的意思。

see eye to eye

兩個人的意見一致。

put the foot down

表明立場或立場堅定。人在態度轉趨強硬時會把本來翹著的腳放下來，暗示接下來要說的話題是嚴肅且正經的，因此這個片語可指「堅定立場」的意思。

stalling
stall (v.) 拖延、擱置。

heads up
(n.) 小心、注意。用來提醒某件事情即將發生。

and all that
其他相關的東西,諸如此類。

make tracks
該動身了,該離開了。

gotta run, catch ya later
我得先去忙,晚點再聊。Gotta 是口語用法,代表我得要,其實就是 "I have got to" 的簡略。Ya = you,是很口語化的說法。

Week 11

Moaning about training
抱怨培訓課程太無聊

Wesley, Dave and Dean are taking a training course given by Eric (Senior HR training manager). However, it is not all as they had hoped for.

衛斯理、戴夫和迪恩正在上艾瑞克（資深人資訓練經理）的培訓課程。然而，卻跟他們預期的有落差。

While Eric is busy giving the training presentation in the conference hall
（艾瑞克正在會議廳忙著培訓講座）

Dean： What time does this **wrap up** at? (checks his phone)

迪恩： 這個幾點**結束**啊？（看手機）

Dave： I don't know but I hope it's soon.

戴夫： 不知道，但我希望早一點。

Wesley： Well I hope this torture, oh sorry I mean training,

can give us **an ace up our sleeves**. He's just reading the information directly from the slides. I mean, come on, we can all read. There's no innovation in this training class at all. It's starting to **cheese me off**.

衛斯理： 嗯，我希望這場折磨，抱歉我是說訓練，可以讓我們**學到一些訣竅**。他只是把投影片唸出來而已。我是說，拜託，我們都識字啊。這堂課一點新意也沒有。**我開始覺得厭煩了。**

Dave： Maybe, who knows? It's been **boring me to tears** the last hour. He will give us a booklet at

the end of the training so we can just read that instead of all this.

戴夫： 也許吧，誰知道？前一小時已經讓我**無聊到流眼淚了**。結束的時候會發一本小手冊，我們自己看就好了，不用坐在這聽他唸。

Dean： I guess we need it to make sure everything is **above board** into the next quarter. **Going forward** we don't want a repeat of the **scandal** that happened in the Finance department. That was **cringe-worthy**.

迪恩： 我想我們要確保一切在進入下一季的時候**清清楚楚**。接下來，我們不希望再看到財務部之前發生的醜聞。真的是想到都會**覺得難堪**。

Wesley： Yeah, we're better than that. At least that's what our reputation says about us.

衛斯理： 對啊，我們可以做得更好的，至少一直以來我們風評都不錯。

Dave： Kill me now! He's talking about rules and regulations. Get me out of here!

戴夫： 殺了我吧！他現在開始講規則和規範。放我出去！

Dean： It can't be much longer. Let's **grin and bear it** together. We're **on the home stretch**.

迪恩： 快結束了啦。**一起忍一忍**就過了。**最後一段**了。

商英譯起來

wrap up

結束、完成、總結。如果跟外國人開會，常會聽到這個說法，表示會議到此結束。"a wrap-up" 則指簡短的結論或摘要，意思與 summary 相同。

an ace up our sleeves

[英式] "an ace up on'e sleeve" 秘笈；錦囊妙計。美式用法則為 "an ace in the hole"。

cheese me off

"cheese sb off"「感到厭煩；惹惱⋯⋯」的意思。cheesy 則代表「劣質、粗俗」的意思，就像品質差的食物，只要裹著滿滿的乳酪，人們還是會被蒙騙而買單。

boring me to tears

"bore sb to tears" 無聊到讓你一直打哈欠流淚。

above board

（計劃或交易）是「誠實、合法」的，在檯面上的。

going forward

未來。後面接著要講的或是發生的事情，可與 next 交替使用。

scandal

(n.) 醜聞，舞弊事件。如果指的是八卦，用 gossip 即可。

cringe worthy

(a.) 令人難堪的、不舒服的。

grin and bear it

grin (v.) 露齒笑。"grin and bear it" 就是笑著忍受，也就是沒有選擇而只能默默接受的意思。

on the home stretch

"home stretch" 距離終點線的最後一段跑道。"on the home stretch" 引申為最後階段，馬上要完成了。

Breakdown in communication while on a business trip
商旅對話頻頻跳針

Dave meets Eric, a Dutch business man while transferring in Dubai airport during a recent business trip. However, Dave is struggling to understand Eric and there is a breakdown in communication at times.

戴夫最近出差，杜拜機場轉機的時候遇到荷蘭商務人士艾瑞克。但是戴夫不太懂艾瑞克的意思，兩人的溝通有時出現理解困難。

Eric： So, what do you do?

艾瑞克： 您在哪高就？

Dave： I'm a sales manager in a multi-national company. And you?

戴夫： 跨國公司的業務經理，您呢？

Eric： Ah yes, nice! I work for myself now in investments and bonds. I used to work for an

NGO, but I **jumped ship** and **went out on my own**. I've **never looked back**! What are you having Dave?

艾瑞克： 啊真好！我自己做投資和債券。我以前在 NGO（非政府組織）上班，後來我**離開了，自己出來創業**。從此**不回頭**！你呢，戴夫？

Dave： Ehh, sorry I'm not sure what you mean?

戴夫： 呃，抱歉，我不太確定你的意思。

Eric： Would you like a drink? Don't worry **it's on me**!

艾瑞克： 你想喝點什麼嗎？別客氣，**我請你**！

Dave： Oh, I don't drink when I'm on business.

戴夫： 喔，我出差不喝酒耶。

Eric： Don't worry. **I won't tell a soul** ha-ha.

艾瑞克： 別擔心，我**不會說出去**的，哈哈。

Dave： You **twisted my arm**. Can I just grab a beer, please?

戴夫： 你**說服我了**。我喝點啤酒好了。

Eric： Sure! So, where are you from?

艾瑞克： 好啊！你從哪裡來的？

Dave： Taiwan. Do you know it? And you, Eric? Is your accent a Swedish one?

戴夫： 台灣。你知道台灣嗎？你呢，艾瑞克？你的口音，是瑞典嗎？

Eric： No, I am Dutch. But I'll **let you away with it**. I've only ever been to Bangkok for business but it was lively.

艾瑞克： 不是，我是荷蘭人，但我大人不記小人過，**放你一馬**。我只去過曼谷出差，蠻有活力的地方。

Dave： Actually, that's Thailand. I'm from Taiwan.

戴夫： 其實曼谷在泰國。我來自台灣。

Eric： Oh, I do apologise Dave. I haven't heard of

Taiwan. What's it famous for? Perhaps you could tell me more about your country before we **part ways**?

艾瑞克： 喔，戴夫，我跟你道歉。我沒聽過台灣。台灣有什麼有名的東西呢？我們**分開**之前可以跟我介紹一下嗎？

Dave： How long do we have? Let's not **lose track of time**...

戴夫： 我們還有多少時間？不要**忘記注意一下時間**……。

ABC 商英譯起來

jumped ship

當同事說要"jump ship"，別擔心！他不是要跳船，而是代表他想要跳槽的意思。

went out on my own

"on my own"代表著自己獨自作業，這裡指跳出來自己創業的意思。

never looked back

"look back"是回憶、回想之意，"never look back"指的是不後悔，永不回頭的意思。

it's on me

我請客、負責的意思。也可以說"My treat."。

won't tell a soul

soul 為靈魂；某種人的意思。"not a soul"就是沒有人的意思。例："There wasn't a soul in that room."。

twisted my arm

扭傷我的手臂，引申為強迫某人做某事的意思。在這裡指「你說動我」的意思。

let you away with it

放你一馬，不追究了。

part ways

分開、分離；意見分歧的意思。例："We part ways on many issues."。

lost track of time

"lose track"是指不知道事情進展到哪，這裡表示未注意到時間。

Offering advice at a family gathering
家族聚會的建議

At a family gathering, Dave discusses his new job and tries his best to **switch off** and enjoy the day. In attendance at the gathering is Alice (Dave's aunt), Frank (Dave's Uncle), Brian (Dave's cousin) and Sophie (Dave's sister).

家族聚會上，戴夫在聊他的新工作，並且試著**徹底放鬆**，享受假日。在場有戴夫的阿姨艾麗斯、舅舅法蘭克、表哥布萊恩和妹妹蘇菲。

Alice： So Dave, **how's the new job treating you**? You look like you **have a lot on your plate** lately!

艾麗斯： 戴夫，新工作**還好嗎**？感覺你最近**事情很多**！

Dave： Ah yeah, not too bad. I've been kind of **stressed out** with the reports and sales figures. The boss is expecting some projections for next week and I'm not sure where I can get them from.

戴夫： 啊，對啊，不錯啦。最近**壓力有點大**，要做報告還

有銷售數據。老闆希望我下禮拜給他的預測報告，
我還不知道要從哪裡生出來。

Sophie：　Let's not **talk shop** on a Sunday while we're
　　　　　having a family lunch alright?

蘇菲：　今天禮拜天，家庭聚餐，不要**聊工作**好嗎？

- -

Frank：　What's this? Are we talking about work again?
　　　　　Let's just enjoy the day and this delicious meal
　　　　　your parents have **rustled up**.

法蘭克：　又來了，又在聊工作？我們好好享受假日，還有
　　　　　你爸媽剛**張羅**好的美食吧！

Dave： Good idea Uncle Frank. Right now, I **don't know whether I'm coming or going.**

戴夫： 舅舅，好主意。我現在有點**不知道在幹嘛**。

Brian： Dave! Step. Away. From. The. Mobile. Phone ha-ha! Don't worry. The company will still survive without you, at least for the afternoon. Sure, you'll be **back to the grindstone** tomorrow anyway so **live a little**. There's more to life than working. It's all about balance.

布萊恩： 戴夫！放下你的手機！放心啦，公司沒有你還是會運轉，至少今天下午不會倒。反正你明天就會進公司**埋頭苦幹**，今天就**好好放鬆地玩**吧。人生不是只有工作。重點是平衡。

Dave： You guys are right, I'm sorry. I've been so **preoccupied** that I've **lost sight of** what's really important to me, and that's you all. Let's **tuck into** this food and relax.

戴夫： 你們說得對，真抱歉。我**太忙了**，**忽略了**真正重要的東西，也就是你們。我們好好**大吃特吃**，放鬆一下吧。

Alice： True. You don't want to **break your back** over

just a job. **At the end of the day**, most of us are **just a number** anyway...

艾麗斯： 是啊。不要為工作**賣掉老命**啦。畢竟**到頭來**，我們也都只是大機器裡的**螺絲釘**⋯⋯。

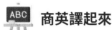 **商英譯起來**

switch off
原指關掉開關的意思，後來引申為不關注周遭、放空的意思。

how's the new job treating you?
新工作還好嗎？也可以說 "How's the new job going?"

have a lot on your plate
plate，「盤子」。盤子上很多東西，意味著事情很多很忙。

stressed out
壓力很大、很焦慮、很緊張。

talk shop
（不用上班的時候）談論工作。

rustled up
張羅，通常指現有的食物做湊合，做成一頓飯。

don't know whether I'm coming or going
不知道要進還是要退，不知所措。

back to the grindstone
重返工作崗位，重新又投入埋頭苦幹。

live a little
盡情享受生活、享受樂趣。

preoccupied

因為過於投入某件事而全神貫注、心事重重的意思。

lost sight of

sight 是視線範圍之處。"lose sight of" 是「忽略、忘記……」的意思。

tuck into

盡情痛快的大吃特吃。

break your back

拼命、賣命的工作。

at the end of the day

到頭來、最終。

just a number

只是一個數字，如眾多螺絲釘般的一顆小角色而已，這裏是勸告戴夫不要把重心都放在工作上，要放鬆一些。

Meetings and Telephone Communication

會議與電話溝通

Setting a goal
定下目標

Dave, Howard, Kate and Sarah have arranged a meeting to discuss the department's strategy for the following quarter.

戴夫、浩爾、凱特和莎拉安排了一場會議，討論他們部門下一季的策略。

Kate： Thanks for taking the time to attend this meeting everyone. I think we are **lagging behind** our competitors these last three months and it is evident in our sales reports. I'm not sure what the main reason is, however, I think we all need to **adhere to** the company's strategic plan.

凱特： 謝謝大家抽空參加這場會議。過去 3 個月我們**被**競爭對手**追上**，從我們的業績報告可以一目了然。我不確定主要原因是什麼，但我想我們都需要**遵從**公司的策略規劃。

Sarah： That all looks very fancy **on paper** Kate, but **it's easier said than done.**

莎拉： 凱特，那些**理論**上能完成都很棒，但**知易行難**。

Kate： And your suggestion is...?

凱特： 那你們有什麼建議呢？

Howard： Okay, let's calm down and just **take a breather** for a few minutes. How about we all set up and implement some personal goals for ourselves and then some for the department which could help us to achieve the strategic plan?

浩爾： 好，我們**冷靜一下**，想個幾分鐘。不如我們各自寫下自己想完成的個人目標，再寫一些能夠幫助我們達成策略規劃的部門目標試試看？

Dave：	**SMART!**
戴夫：	**SMART!**
Howard：	Thanks Dave, I think so too!
浩爾：	謝啦，戴夫，我也覺得！

Dave：	No, I mean we must establish goals that are Specific, Measurable, Achievable, Realistic, and Time based.
戴夫：	不是啦，我是說我們應該建立符合 SMART 原則的目標：明確、可量化、可達成、符合現況，且可在時間內達成。
Kate：	I guess that wouldn't be the worst idea.
凱特：	還不錯的想法。

Howard：	We have to stop **throwing caution to the wind** because **going forward** we need **to bolster** these sales figures and increase our client base.
浩爾：	我們應該不要再**魯莽行事**，因為**接下來**我們需要**加強**銷售數據，增加客戶量。

Sarah：	Sounds good to me. When shall we **pencil** this SMART goal setting deadline **in** for?
莎拉：	聽起來不錯喔。我們這個 SMART 目標要**訂在**什麼

時間之前完成？

Dave： Next week would be ideal for me. I got some clients **in town** till Friday evening.

戴夫： 下禮拜蠻理想的。我客戶會**來找我**，他們待到這週五傍晚。

Howard： Okay, let's agree to get these goals finished by next Wednesday. I **gotta** get back to my desk. **Keep** me **posted** guys.

Howard leaves in a hurry to get back to his desk.
（浩爾迅速回到他的位子）

浩爾： 好，我們一起在下週三前把目標訂出來。我**得**先回座位忙了，有**新消息**跟我說。

Sarah： **The show must go on!**

莎拉： **該做的事還是得先完成！**

商英譯起來

lagging behind

"lag behind"，是「落後、脫隊」；（相較於其他人）移動緩慢的意思。

adhere to

遵守，忠於。

on paper

理論上來說；書面上看來的意思，也就是紙上談兵。

it's easier said than done

說的比做的簡單，也就是知易行難的意思。

take a breather

Breather (n.)，短暫休息的意思。"Take a deep breath"則是大口深呼吸的樣子，通常用在舒緩緊張。

SMART

此為 (Specific, Measurable, Attainable, Realistic, Time-based) 五個單字的縮寫，意指目標必須是具體的、可衡量的、可達到的、符合現況的，以及有明確截止期限的。

throwing caution to the wind

caution 是小心謹慎的意思，"throw caution to the wind"指把謹慎隨手拋到風中，指不顧風險，魯莽行事的意思。

going forward

= "in the future"，未來的意思。後面接著要講的或是發生的事情。

to bolster

提高，改善，與 improve 意義相近。

pencil... in

"pencil sth in" 指用鉛筆暫時寫下來，之後也可做更改，是暫定安排的意思。而 "pencil sb in" 則是先幫某人預約（門診或會面）的意思。另一句和 pencil 相關的片語也很重要，"sharpen your pencil"，這可不是叫你削鉛筆，而是你的廠商想要你「降價」！

in town

當說話者說 "someone is in town" 指的是他人來到自己的居住地，比如文中提到有客戶會 "in town"，就是會來拜訪自己的意思。

keep me posted

"keep sb posted" 是告訴某人最新情況的意思。

gotta

"have got to" 的簡略用法，是連音而成，指「必須、得要……」的意思。

the show must go on

不管發生什麼事，戲都要演下去，指不論遇到什麼困難，事情一樣得做。

Hiring a foreign language tutor for staff

僱用培訓員工的語言老師

Chloe from the Human Resources (HR) Department has scheduled a meeting with Dave, Howard and Dean to help her pick the best candidate for the new business language tutor position. Going forward, Chloe and the attendees of the meeting feel they need to upskill their workforce, **seeing as** a majority of their business is in Germany and Canada.

人資的克蘿伊已安排跟戴夫、浩爾和迪恩開會，討論如何挑選新的商務語言教師。展望未來，克蘿伊和其他與會同事認為他們需要提升自己的工作能力，因為**考慮到**公司多數業務在德國和加拿大。

Chloe： Should we **go with** this guy here? We could **kill two birds with one stone** here because he is a **Germany** and English business language trainer. It could be better as we could negotiate a slightly cheaper fee. It may **save us a bundle**.

克蘿伊：　我們應該**選**這位嗎？**一石二鳥**，因為他同時是**德國人**，也是英文商務語言訓練師。若能跟他談到優惠一點的價錢就好了。可以幫我們**省下不少費用**。

Chloe shows the guys a CV of the potential candidate
（克蘿伊把候選人的履歷秀給大家看）

Dean：　I think you mean German language trainer, right?

迪恩：　妳是指德文老師，對吧？

Chloe：　You're right, I always get those mixed up, sorry. I guess it wouldn't hurt for me to **get a taster** of some new business English terms.

克蘿伊：　對，我每次都搞錯，抱歉。我想，**試著使用**一些新的商務英文詞彙也不錯吧。

Dave： I'm intrigued. He's **the best out of a bad bunch**.

戴夫： 好有趣，他是候選人裡面**素質還算可以的一個**。

Howard： Well, he claims to use **an AI assisted teaching assistant** in his classes. Another thing worth noting with this candidate is that he only accepts payment via Bitcoin. Are we comfortable doing that and do we have our Bitcoin account established yet?

浩爾： 嗯，他說他上課會使用到 **AI 人工智慧助理**來輔助教學。另一點值得注意的是他只接受比特幣付款。我們可以接受嗎？我們的比特幣帳戶開了沒？

Dean： **I'm on it.**

迪恩： **我來處理。**

Chloe： Are you sure you can handle this?

克蘿伊： 你確定你可以嗎？

Dean： Don't worry. It's **not my first rodeo**.

迪恩： 放心，我**不是菜鳥**。

Dave： Oh yeah, I forgot Bitcoin is **your forté**.

戴夫： 喔，好耶，我都忘記你對比特幣**很了解**。

Chloe： It's a **sticking point** for me guys if I'm being honest. All this talk of an A.I. teaching assistant and payment via Bitcoin just gives me **butterflies**.

克蘿伊： 老實說，我**不太能接受**耶。講這些人工智慧助理啊，比特幣支付什麼的，讓我怪**緊張**的。

Dean： Come on, let's **get with the times!** Cash payments are **so last year.**

迪恩： 拜託，我們要**跟上潮流！**現金支付已經**過時**了。

Howard： I think if we can get him at a reasonable price then let's go with him.

浩爾： 我覺得如果可以跟他談到合理價格，就用他吧。

Dave： Yeah, I agree with Howard on this Chloe. Let's go with him!

戴夫： 對啊，我同意浩爾的想法，克蘿伊。就用他啊。

Chloe： Okay, I'll get him in for an interview on Tuesday. **Sorted!**

克蘿伊： 好，我請他週二來面試。**搞定！**

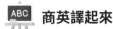 **商英譯起來**

seeing as...

"seeing as/ that...",「考慮到……」;「既然……」的意思,後面接句子當連接詞使用。意思與 since 一樣。

go with this guy

"go with sb/ sth",選某人或某物的意思。

kill two birds with one stone

一石二鳥,事半功倍。

*Germany

德國 (在文中 Chloe 將德文 German 錯用為德國 Germany)。

save us a bundle

bundle 是一大捆、大束的意思,"a bundle"口語可用來指「一大筆錢」。"save us a bundle"就是幫我們省一大筆錢,"make/ cost a buddle"則是 「賺大錢 / 花了一筆錢」的意思。

to get a taster

taster (n.) 可以嚐試的新事物。

the best out of a bad bunch

在一群品質尚可的人或物中,勉強選出來比較好的一個,也就是從一堆爛蘋果中選出一顆比較不爛的。

an AI assisted teaching assistant

AI 就是 "Artificial Intelligence" 人工智慧的縮寫，"AI assisted teaching assistant" 人工智慧教學助理，為一種虛擬的教學軟體系統。

I'm on it .

我來處理；交給我吧，指主動負責解決某任務或問題。

not my first rodeo

rodeo 是指牛仔競技表演，這裡用來告訴別人他們所說的你都知道，自己並不是新手的意思。

your forté

forté (n.) 強項、專長。

sticking point

（討論中意見不同）分歧點；癥結。

butterflies

胃裡面在攪動像蝴蝶拍動翅膀，就是（對即將要做的事）感到很不安、很緊張。

get with the times

跟上潮流，知道並會調整腳步跟上最近的趨勢。

sorted

sorted (a.) 準備好了；解決了。

Discussing how to increase consumer base
討論如何增加客戶量

Dean, Howard, and Wesley discuss issues **relating to** the company's CRM in a meeting at the recreation area by the coffee counter.

迪恩、浩爾和衛斯理在咖啡台旁的公共娛樂區，討論與公司客戶關係

Wesley： Guys, I was examining the data from our Zeeko CRM system and we have been losing customers recently. We are letting them **slip through our fingers** when we should be holding onto them. Where are we going wrong?

衛斯理： 夥伴們，我剛在看我們 Zeeko 客戶關係管理系統的數據，發現最近流失了一些客戶。那些客戶是我們該留住的，但卻**留不住**他們。我們的策略方針到底哪裡出錯？

Howard： I think one reason is that our price has remained the same for two years whereas our main competitors are offering the same solutions but at a lower price. We must **take a long hard look at** ourselves and decide how we can provide more value to our **clientele**.

浩爾： 我想其中一個原因是我們過去兩年價格都沒調整，而我們的競爭對手卻提供了相同的解決方案，但價格卻比我們更低。我們一定要**好好檢討**自我反省，想辦法為**客戶群**提供更多價值。

Wesley： An option would be to provide some training to our associated teams. That way we can get them **up to speed** with the system. This will help them improve their selling and support capabilities.

衛斯理： 可以考慮提供我們的夥伴團隊一些訓練。如此就可以讓他們**跟上**系統的**進度**。幫助他們改善銷售和支援的能力。

Dean： I agree, Wesley. Previously, we have been **putting all our eggs in one basket** and it looks like that was a risky move.

迪恩： 我同意。之前我們都**把雞蛋放在同一個籃子裡**，風險真是很高。

Howard： It was. How about we implement an automated feedback survey for our customers? That way we can better understand our consumer's behaviour. You know what they say: **"knowledge is power"**.

浩爾： 的確。我們來做個客戶自動回饋調查系統如何？這樣我們可以更了解消費者的行為模式。你知道大家都怎麼說的，**「知識就是力量」**。

Dean： Nice idea. Combine that with the staff training and I think we can **get back on track**. Now we just have the price issue to deal with. We ought to do something about it.

迪恩： 好主意。這可以跟員工訓練並行，這樣我們就可以**重回正軌**。現在我們只要處理定價問題就好。必須好好處理。

Howard： True. It's time we stopped **playing the waiting game** and acted. But, I think the price problem is another day's work.

浩爾： 沒錯。我們該停止**觀望**，開始行動了。但我想價格問題要再擇日討論。

Wesley： Okay, are we all agreed? Does anyone have any qualms about this?

衛斯理： 好的，我們都同意嗎？大家還有什麼問題？

Dean & Howard： Fine with us.

迪恩 & 浩爾： 沒問題。

🖥 商英譯起來

relating to...
與……有關。

slip through our fingers
（因為不夠努力或謹慎）讓機會錯過。

take a long hard look at...
為了將來更好的進步，而審視、檢視。

clientele
常光顧的一群忠實顧客、客戶，為主顧客、常客的意思。單數則為 client，有客戶；顧客的意思，可指買商品或買服務的客人。customer 則較偏向購買實體商品的顧客。

up to speed
了解最新情況並且跟上進度，但通常與速度無直接關聯。

putting all our eggs in one basket
雞蛋放在同一個籃子裡，風險極高！

knowledge is power
知識就是力量，亦即了解越多，勝算越多。

get back on track
重新返回軌道，追回流失的客戶量。

playing the waiting game

先觀望，後行動，伺機而動的意思。

qualms

qualm (n.) 疑慮；不安之意，不確定是否在做對的事。

Week 17

Making a conference call
電話會議

In a recent **conference call** meeting; Dave is struggling to understand Gertz and Rajesh; his co-workers **based in** Germany and India. Sarah is also in the meeting room to oversee the proceedings.

電話會議中。戴夫很難了解格茨和拉傑什在說什麼，這兩位同事分別**駐點**在德國和印度。莎拉也在會議室中監控會議進行。

Rajesh： We want to expand our sales here in India by 15% over the next three quarters. Is this **doable** brother Dave?

拉傑什： 我們希望在未來三季時間讓印度的銷售額成長15%。你覺得**可行**嗎，戴夫兄弟？

Dave： I'm sorry could you say that again Rajesh, **I didn't catch that.**

戴夫： 抱歉，可以再說一次嗎，拉傑什？我**沒聽到你剛剛說什麼**。

- -

Rajesh： Yes Mr. Dave. Can you hear me? I hope our branch here in India can increase our sales by 15% over the next three quarters. Can we do this?

拉傑什： 好的，戴夫先生。聽得清楚嗎？我希望我們的印度分公司在接下來三季銷售額可以提高 15%。我們做得到嗎？

Dave： I think it may be a little too optimistic, but we can aim for that figure. What's **the lay of the land** like in Cologne, Gertz?

戴夫： 我認為可能有點過度樂觀，但我們可以把這數字作為目標。 格茨和科隆**目前的狀況**如何？

Gertz： Yes, Dave we are performing at optimal levels here in Germany. We saw a small **dip** in performance back in **Q1** however, we feel that was due to a Christmas and New Year **lull**. Can you **capitalize on** this **momentum** Dave?

格茨： 是的，戴夫，我們在德國表現目前形勢樂觀。雖然**第一季**業績略有**下降**，但我們認為那是聖誕節和新年前**暫時的景氣低迷**。你能好好**利用**年節前這個**時機點賺錢**嗎，戴夫？

Dave： Gertz, can you hear me? I think we have a poor connection. What was that you said about Christmas?

戴夫： 格茨，聽得到嗎？收訊很糟。你剛說聖誕節什麼？

Gertz： The slow sales figures were a representation of people's **lack of funds** over the Christmas period. That is **the only thing** I can **put it down to.**

格茨： 低迷的銷售數據代表的是大家在聖誕節期間**缺乏資金**。這是我唯一可以**想到的原因**。

Dave： I understand Gertz, thanks for your feedback. We are doing quite well here however, we could be doing better.

戴夫： 我了解，格茨，謝謝你的回應。我們這裡現在狀況還不錯，不過還可以更好。

Rajesh： We aim for 15% Mr. Dave, sir?

拉傑什： 我們目標是 15% 對吧，戴夫先生？

Dave： Let's aim for that yes, Rajesh. Can we schedule another call for two weeks later with an update?

戴夫： 是的，我們先定下這樣的目標吧，拉傑什。我們可以安排兩週後電話回報新消息嗎？

Gertz： Let's hope the connection improves for our next meeting Dave.

格茨： 希望我們下次開會連線品質會比較好，戴夫。

Dave： Absolutely. Thank you both for your time. I will forward a reminder onto you both to sync your calendars. Goodbye.

戴夫： 當然。謝謝你們撥冗。我會把開會提醒轉發給你們兩位，讓你們行事曆可以同步。再見。

Rajesh： Bye for now, brother Dave.

拉傑什： 再見啦，戴夫兄弟。

Gertz disconnects without saying goodbye
*** 格茨沒說再見就斷線了 ***

Dave turns to Sarah after the conference call is finished
*** 戴夫在會議結束後去找莎拉 ***

Dave： I had **a knot in my stomach** for all of that con-call meeting. I had to pretend the connection was poor to give me time to **register** what they were saying.

戴夫： 我開這種電話會議**胃都緊張到快打結了**。我還得假裝收訊不好，爭取時間**注意**他們到底在說什麼。

Sarah： Don't worry, you'll **get the hang of it**!

莎拉： 放心，你會**抓到訣竅**的！

ABC 商英譯起來

conference call
電話會議，三個人以上的電話會談。

based in
"be based in ..." 指「工作駐點在……」的意思。

doable
"able to be done"，可行；行的通。

didn't catch that
在對方敘述事情時，沒有聽清楚或不理解的意思。

the lay of the land
「地勢、地形」，引申做情勢、情況。

dip
短暫的下降，dip 也有沾或者在液體浸一下的意思。

Q1
第一季。一年有四季，quarter 這個字為四分之一，商業用語也就將 Q1~Q4 訂為四季訂定目標時的縮寫；而 Q1 就是第一季的意思。

lull
短暫的停擺；不景氣。

capitalize on

利用局勢，從中獲益、賺錢。

momentum

契機，動力。

lack of funds

資金不足。"lack of"可以接在各種詞彙的前面，強調其匱乏性，比如 "lack of food"，食物不夠，或是"lack of sleep"，睡眠不足。

the only thing I can put it down to

"put sth down to sth"把某事當作造成某事的原因，本對話中的"the only thing I can put it down to"是這是我唯一想到造成的原因的意思。常用"put it down to experience"為把某事看作是一次可學習的教訓。

a knot in my stomach

胃糾在一起，表很緊張的意思。

get the hang of it

hang 是掌握或把握住。"get the hang of it"指學會做某件事，也就是抓到訣竅的意思。

Week 18

Late for a meeting
開會遲到

Dave joins the meeting just as it is **wrapping up**. Kevin, one of the senior managers, **has a go at** Dave after Dave enters the room.

戴夫加入時，會議已經**即將結束**。高階經理凱文在戴夫一進會議室時，對戴夫**砲轟**。

Kevin： Dave, I **have a bone to pick with you**! What time do you call this? You think you can just come **sauntering** in to this meeting whenever you like? Huh? You're 30 minutes late and that simply isn't good enough.

凱文： 戴夫，我得要**說說你**！現在幾點了？你覺得這個會議是隨你想幾點就幾點**晃**進來的嗎？啊？你遲到了三十分鐘，這是完全不能接受的。

Dave： I am very sorry Kevin. I got delayed coming bac-...

戴夫： 凱文，非常抱歉。我被耽誤了，回來的時……

Kevin： I don't want to hear your excuses, **I've had it up to here with** them. This isn't the first time you've been late to a meeting.

凱文： 我不想聽你的藉口，**我受夠了**。這不是你第一次開會遲到了。

Dave： I know, it's just that I couldn't ge-...

戴夫： 我知道，我就是沒辦法……

Kevin： **Save your breath** Dave! You're late and now you want to waste all of our time? **Do you think I came down in the last shower?** Get out of my sight!

凱文： **省點力氣吧**，戴夫！你遲到了，現在還想浪費我們所有人的時間嗎？**你覺得我新來的嗎？**滾出我的視線！

Dave： My apologies Kevin.

戴夫： 凱文，我非常抱歉。

Kevin： Come see me in the morning at 9am, not a second later.

凱文： 明天早上九點整來找我，不能遲到。

***Dave turns and whispers to Wesley as he is leaving the meeting room to express his frustration with the situation. ***
*** 戴夫離開會議室後，跟衛斯理小聲表達他的沮喪。***

Dave： Jeez, I didn't know he **had a short fuse**.

戴夫： 老天，我不知道他**這麼容易發飆**。

Wesley： **You're in the bad books** now. Good luck!

衛斯理： **你被凱文記住**了。祝你好運！

🔤 商英譯起來

wrap up

結束、完成。跟外國人開會，常會聽到這個說法表示會議到此為止結束。
"a wrap-up" 則指簡短的摘要或結論，意思與 summary 相同。

has a go at Dave

"have a go at sb" 針對某人砲轟、批評。

have a bone to pick with you

" have a bone to pick with sb" 對某人有意見；向某人抱怨。

sauntering

saunter (v.) 閒逛、漫步，沒有特定的目的地。

I've had it up to here with them

"have had it (up to here) with..." 有「對……已經忍到極限了」；「受夠了……」的意思，也可以用 "be fed up with..."。

save your breath

省省力氣吧，做什麼人家都不會相信你了。也可以用 "don't waste your breath"。

Do you think I came down in the last shower?

"I didn't come down in the last shower." 別把我當傻子，為澳洲用法，意思為告知對方勿把自己當外行或是菜鳥。

had a short fuse

fuse 是導火線的意思，短的導火線容易引燃。所以 "have a short fuse" 指的是易怒的意思。

you're in the bad books

"in sb's bad/ good books" 被某人厭惡 / 喜歡。

Business Negotiations
協商

Dean and Wesley are deep into a con-call negotiation meeting with Mr. Tino, a potential client who wants to get the best deal.

迪恩和衛斯理正埋頭和提諾先生開電話會議，提諾先生是位潛在客戶，他想談到一個好價錢。

Dean： We understand your concerns Mr. Tino, however, we can assure you our quality is superior to that of our nearest competitor and everything is **above board** on our side.

迪恩： 提諾先生，我們了解你的考量。但是，我們可以跟您保證，我們的品質優於其他同業，一切都**公開透明**。

Mr. Tino： You know, I could get my order for 6% less if I **go elsewhere**?

提諾先生： 你知道，在**別處**我可以用便宜 6% 的價格購買嗎？

Wesley： We know, but don't believe everything you hear Mr. Tino, their quality is not the same. They have been **cutting corners** ever since they moved their manufacturing unit to India. The difference is obvious. We could **come down** by 2% to help you make this decision.

衛斯理： 我們知道，但提諾先生，您不能相信所有聽到的事，他們跟我們的品質一定有差。自從他們家把生產線移到印度，就一直**偷工減料**。差異顯而易見。為了讓您比較好做決定，我們可以**再優惠** 2%。

Mr. Tino： **If you play your cards right** and reduce your final figure by 6% then the deal is on. I'm **on a tight budget** this year.

提諾先生： 如果你**處理得好**，總數再便宜 6% 給我，我們就成交。我今年**預算比較緊**。

Dean： That's **out of the question!** Let's **meet halfway** and secure this order with a reduction of our initial price by 4%? Let's **put this negotiation to bed**.

迪恩： **不可能！**我們**各退一步**了，訂價我可以優惠您4%？我們**就這樣講定**吧。

Mr. Tino： You guys know how to **play hard ball**! I'm happy with that compromise.

提諾先生： 你們**很懂硬派作法**！這樣的調整我可以接受。

Wesley： Great to hear! I'll have my secretary send your **PA** a confirmation contract and the related documents.

衛斯理： 太好了！我請秘書把確認合約和相關文件寄給您**助理**。

Mr. Tino： Perfecto, **Ciao** guys!

提諾先生： 完美。各位**再見**啦！

商英譯起來

above board

都在檯面上進行，公開透明；公正無欺。

elsewhere

（adv.）在別處；去別處。

cutting corners

"cut corners" 偷工減料；抄捷徑。

come down

降價，優惠。

if you play your cards right

如果你處理得宜、計畫得當。

on a tight budget

預算不夠；資金不夠。

out of the question

impossible，不可能的意思。

meet halfway

halfway（adv.）在中間；中途。"meet (sb) halfway" 指（與某人）妥協，各退一步的意思。

put this negotiation to bed

"put sth to bed" 解決某事了；(討論、思考) 到此結束。

to play hardball

hardball (n.) 棒球，"play hardball" 是採取強硬的做法的意思。

PA

"personal assistant" 的縮寫，個人助理。

ciao

Good-bye，義大利語。美國人口語常用。

Acting on a security breach
改善安全漏洞

Jack, Head of Security based in Stockholm, Sweden has called a con-call meeting with Dave, Kate and Howard about a recent **security breach** in the company.

瑞典斯德哥爾摩的安全部門主管傑克,與戴夫、凱特和浩爾召開電話會議,討論公司內部最近一次**保安系統的漏洞**。

Jack： Right now, we are in **uncharted territory** as we have never had a breach like this.

傑克： 現在,我們面臨著**陌生的新狀況**,過去從來沒遇過這樣的漏洞。

Kate： What exactly happened, Jack?

凱特： 到底發生什麼事了,傑克?

- -

Jack： Our security technicians informed me yesterday that an unknown source **infiltrated** our

anti-hacking software system and entered our database. They **ransacked** 80% of our customers' details.

傑克： 昨天我們的安全技術人員通知我，一個不明來源**侵入**進我們的**防駭軟體**，進入資料庫，**劫取**了我們八成客戶的資訊。

Howard： Are there any solutions to this **dicey** situation?

浩爾： 有什麼辦法能解決這種**風險**？

Jack： We must improve our security software system and **put** this sensitive information **out of harm's way**.

傑克： 我們一定要改善資安軟體系統，**保障這些**敏感資訊的**安全**。

Dave： We are **sitting ducks**! We should have used **Blockchain** technology.

戴夫： 我們簡直是駭客的**活靶**！應該早點用**區塊鏈**科技才對。

Jack： Bit late now, eh? But, I think going forward we need to utilise this technology to be **on the safe side**.

傑克： 有點晚了嗎？但是，我想接下來，我們需要好好善用這項技術，**以防萬一**。

Kate： Let's **lock that in**, Jack, and we can go from there. Have your guys make the changes and we will schedule a call for next week to assess the situation. Thanks.

凱特： 傑克，我們**快改善**吧，再由此調整。請你們團隊再改善，我們會再安排一次會議做現況評估，謝謝。

ABC 商英譯起來

a security breach

breach (n.) 破壞；違反 (合約、規定)，"security breach" 則指保全的漏洞。

uncharted territory

uncharted (a.)，全新的；無人涉足的；territory (n.) 領域。

infiltrated

滲透、侵入。

anti-hacking

hack (v.) 侵入 / 駭入 電腦系統 (未經允許)。字首 anti- 是「反」的意思，所以 anti-hacking 是反駭客；而 anti-clockwise 就是逆時針方向的意思。

ransacked

ransack (v.) 搶劫；掠奪；粗魯地翻搜。

dicey

dice 是骰子的意思，擲骰子決定則表情況不可靠，所以 dicey 為有風險的意思。

put...out of harm's way

把……安置到安全的地方；避開危險。

sitting ducks

活靶；易被擊中的目標，也就是指好騙，容易擊倒的人。

blockchain

區塊鏈，是藉由密碼學串連，可保護內容的串連交易記錄（又稱區段）。

(just) to be on the safe side

謹慎起見，以防萬一。

lock that in

"lock sth in" 做某事以期得到改善。

Week 21

Week 21

Making a workplace disabled-friendly

無障礙的工作環境

Dean, Howard, and Wesley are in a con-call meeting with the local city council trying to arrange the implementation of a disabled-friendly working environment. Michael is one of the civil servants from the council on the other end of the call.

迪恩、浩爾和衛斯理正在和當地的市議會進行電話會議，討論無障礙工作環境的施行細節。電話另一頭是市議會的公務人員麥可。

Dean： Michael we are at a stage now where we need to make **reasonable adjustments** to our office. Ignorance is not the attitude we want to take and we hope you can help us with this process. It's **a no-brainer** that we need to change.

迪恩： 麥可，我們辦公室的環境現階段需要**做一些需要的調整**。我們不想草率行事，希望您能夠協助我們。**無疑地**，我們絕對需要調整。

Michael： Absolutely, have you applied for the permits and planning permission?

麥可： 那是絕對的。請問您申請施工和規劃許可了嗎？

Howard： We have indeed. Have you received them? **We're asking for trouble** if we don't make a change.

浩爾： 已經申請了。請問您有收到嗎？如果我們不調整現況，就是在**自找麻煩**。

Michael： I can see them on the system now. It says here that you want a wheelchair ramp, and improvements made in the bathrooms?

麥可： 我在系統上看到了。你們寫到需要輪椅坡道，還有廁所需要改善施工，對嗎？

Wesley： Correct!

衛斯理： 是的！

Michael： It all looks fine however, **the crux of the matter** is the time issue. It may take up to nine months for the planning permission to be granted.

麥可： 一切看起來都沒問題，不過，**主要問題**是時間。規劃許可可能要花九個月才會核可完成。

Dean： Is there any way we can speed up this **teething problem** to make the changes happen sooner?

迪恩： 有沒有其他方法可以讓這些**問題**早點解決，早點開工嗎？

Michael： **In a word**, no! The only thing we can do now is wait. These things take time and we have to **go with the flow**.

麥可： **一句話**，不行！現在我們所能做的就是等待。就是需要時間，我們就**順其自然**吧。

Wesley： Let's not **ruffle any feathers**, then. We'll **touch base** next month!

衛斯理： 不要**讓任何一方不開心**啦。下個月再**討論**吧！

商英譯起來

reasonable adjustments
合理範圍內的調整。

a no-brainer
不須加以思考的事;不用多想就知道答案的事。

we're asking for trouble
" be asking for trouble"自找麻煩;自討苦吃的意思。

the crux of the matter
crux (n.) 癥結;關鍵。"the crux of the matter"指的是事件的核心問題。

teething problem
"teething problem" 或 "teething trouble"事情發生初期所遇到的麻煩或棘手之處。

in a word
簡單來說,一言以蔽之。

go with the flow
順其自然;順應潮流;隨波逐流。

ruffle any feathers
ruffle 是弄亂、使不順的意思,把平順的羽毛弄亂了,人家當然要生氣了。
"ruffle sb's feathers"指使某人生氣或心煩意亂的意思。

touch base
(用開會或說話的方式)了解對方的想法;得知最新的消息。

Week 22
A team building event
團契活動

Dave, Kate and Wesley are in a meeting to arrange a team building event for the staff. They hope to have it outdoors to make it fun and exciting for their colleagues.

戴夫、凱特和衛斯理正開會安排員工的團隊默契活動。他們希望活動能安排在戶外，同事會覺得比較有趣和刺激。

Kate： **Feast your eyes on this**, guys!

凱特： 嘿大家，**快來欣賞一下**！

Wesley： What are we looking at here?

衛斯理： 什麼這麼好看？

Kate shows the others a brochure
凱特給大家看一本手冊

Kate： What better way to **blow away the cobwebs** than a team building weekend in the mountains?

凱特： 有什麼比到山裡舉辦團隊默契活動更能**提振**大家的 **精神**呢？

Dave： Isn't it a little far away? I mean, it looks good but it also looks like we have to set up our own tents? I didn't **sign up for this!**

戴夫： 不會有點遠嗎？我是說，看起來不錯，但我們好像 要自己搭帳棚？我可沒有**報名參加這種活動**喔！

Wesley： No, look! The company takes care of everything for us. We'll **have a ball**. So, we head down there after work on Friday, right?

衛斯理： 不是，你看！負責公司會把一切都處理好。我們會**玩得很開心**的。所以我們週五下班直接出發，對嗎？

Kate： Yep, that's the plan. Then, after the day of activities on Saturday, we can all **paint the town red**.

凱特： 對，是這樣規劃。禮拜六全天活動之後，我們可以**盡情狂歡**一番。

Dave： Now, that's **more my cup of tea**!

戴夫： 現在講的**正中我下懷**呢！

Wesley： What does it say here about Sunday's plan? There's going to be river tracing and abseiling? Howard and Dean will be **in their element**.

衛斯理： 行程上週日的規劃是什麼？溯溪和繩降？浩爾和迪恩應該會**如魚得水**。

Dave： I think you've **twisted my arm**, Kate. I'm happy to go with that idea.

戴夫： 你**說服我了**，凱特。就照計畫走吧。

Kate： Sounds good, right? The only thing is the price.

凱特： 聽起來不錯，對吧？就差在價錢了。

Wesley： **What's the damage?**

衛斯理： **要花多少錢？**

Kate： It's working out around $7,500USD.

凱特： 差不多是七千五百美元。

Dave： Well, I hope it's worth it!

戴夫： 嗯，希望值得囉！

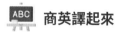 **商英譯起來**

feast your eyes on this

"feast your eyes on..." 盡情欣賞，大飽眼福的意思。

blow away the cobwebs

cobweb 是蜘蛛網的意思，把蜘蛛網吹掉，引申為把疲勞、煩躁一掃而空的，也就是消除疲勞；振作精神的意思。

sign up for this

"sign up for..."，「報名參加 ⋯⋯」的意思。

have a ball

好好地玩；盡情狂歡。

paint the town red

飲酒作樂、跳舞；熱鬧狂歡。19 世紀時，英國一個愛無事生非的侯爵在某個晚上把鎮上的幾棟房子漆成了紅色，現在衍生成大肆狂歡的意思，並且活動中通常包括酒精的存在。

more my cup of tea

就是我喜歡的事；就是我擅長的事。

in their element

element (n.) 適合某人的環境或事物。"be sb's element" 表示 (對某事) 得心應手；(在某地) 適得其所的意思。

twisted my arm

扭傷我的手臂，引申為強迫某人做某事的意思。在此是指說服你的意思。

What's the damage?

damage 通常是傷害的意思，不過 "the damage" 在這裡代表的是某物所花的費用。

Week 23

Customer's problem-solving over the phone
電話上解決顧客問題

Sarah takes a call from an impatient customer and there appears to be some miscommunication during the telephone call.

莎拉接到一通顧客的電話，顧客有些不耐煩，在電話中雙方有些許的誤會。

Sarah： Good morning, Sarah speaking. How may I-

莎拉： 早安，我是莎拉。有什麼需要我 ---

Customer **cuts Sarah off** before she can finish her sentence
*** 莎拉還沒說完，顧客就**打斷她說話**了 ***

Customer： Yes who is this?

顧客： 請問你是？

Sarah： This is Sarah.

莎拉： 我是莎拉。

Customer： I **heard through the grapevine** you will have a sale starting on the 5th of June. Is this right?

顧客： **聽說**六月五日開始你們會有特價活動。是嗎？

Sarah： I am sorry sir, I don't know. I don't work in that department. I can transf-

莎拉： 先生，很抱歉我並不清楚此事，我不在那個部門工作。我可以幫你轉 ---

Customer： What? But, I heard you'll have the summer sale starting on the 5th?

顧客： 妳說什麼？但我聽說從五號開始，妳們會有夏季特惠的活動？

Sarah： The only thing I can tell you is that we have a 10% discount on all purchases made online.

莎拉： 我只知道，所有網購將會有 10% 的折扣。

Customer： That's still a **rip-off**! I want the full 50% sale!

顧客： 那還是**貴得離譜**！我要求 50% 折扣！

Sarah： I can understand, sir. Like I mentioned, I don't know because I don't work in that department so, I cannot tell you the exact information.

莎拉： 先生，我了解。誠如我所說的，我不在那個部門工作，所以無法告知您確切的資訊。

Customer： Well, who can I speak to who knows the **ins and outs** of the summer sale? This is taking too long. **I don't have all day**.

顧客： 好吧，哪位工作人員可以跟我說夏季特惠的**細節內容**？我們已經講太久了，**我可沒那閒工夫**。

Sarah： Certainly Sir, thank you for your patience. Let me transfer you to the correct department for this query.

莎拉： 沒問題，先生。感謝您的耐心等候，我將為您轉接到該部門來回應您的問題。

Sarah transfers the customer to the correct department and sighs with relief
*** 莎拉將客戶轉接至該部門，如釋重負地鬆了口氣。***

商英譯起來

cuts Sarah off

"cut sb off" 為打斷某人說話的意思。

heard through the grapevine

"hear sth through/ on the grapevine" 透過小道消息聽到；口耳相傳。
grapevine 是葡萄藤，既然是穿越層層葡萄藤聽到的，表示非透過正式的
消息傳遞。

rip-off

索價過高的物品。

the ins and outs

來龍去脈，要做好某件事情或工作所需具備的細節。

I don't have all day

表現不耐煩的語氣，請對方別拖拖拉拉的，沒有多餘的空閒時間能等他的
意思。

Making an excuse while on a call

打電話時編造藉口

Audrey, the receptionist, has taken a call. The caller is looking to speak to Dean, who is in the office, but, would rather not take the call.

接待員奧黛麗接到一通打給迪恩的電話。迪恩在辦公室，但他不想接這通電話。

Caller： Hi, can I speak to Dean?

對方： 嗨，請問迪恩方便接電話嗎？

Audrey： Who's calling, please?

奧黛麗： 請問您是？

Caller： It's Mr. Robinson from Traveltech. He should **be expecting** my call. I've been trying to **get hold of** him but he is a hard man to **track down**.

對方： 我是 Traveltech 的羅賓森，他應該**知道**我會打來。我嘗試**聯繫**他好幾次了，但很難**找到**他。

Audrey： **Just a minute**, let me check and see if he's in the office.

奧黛麗： **請稍候**，我確認一下他是否在辦公室。

Audrey puts Mr. Robinson on hold and looks over at Dean's desk
*** 奧黛麗讓羅賓森稍候片刻，並去迪恩的辦公桌找他 ***

Audrey： I have a call from Mr. Robinson for you. Would you like to take it? He says **you've been out of touch** with him recently.

奧黛麗： 有位羅賓森先生打來找你，需要幫你轉接嗎？他說他最近都**連絡不上**你。

Dean gestures to Audrey to show he is not here by air swiping his hand across his neck
*** 迪恩在空氣中比著用手劃過脖子的手勢，示意奧黛麗說他不在 ***

Dean： No. I haven't **wrapped up** the contract agreement with them yet, so, **make something up**. I'll get back to him tomorrow.

迪恩： 不，他們的合約我還沒**完成**。先給他**編個藉口**，我明天再聯繫他。

Audrey： Sure, **no dramas**.

奧黛麗： 好的，**沒問題**。

Audrey： Thanks for your patience Mr. Robinson. Dean has just gone into a meeting. His schedule is **chock-a-block** today but, he will **be in touch with** you first thing tomorrow morning.

奧黛麗： 感謝您的等候，羅賓森先生。迪恩剛去開會了，他今天**行程滿檔**。但他明早一早**會優先聯絡**你。

Caller： Okay, thanks for that. Bye.

對方： 好的，感謝你。再見。

ABC 商英譯起來

expect
(v.) 知道某人會來或某事會發生。

get hold of
"get hold of sb"，試著聯絡上某人。

track down
追蹤到；找到。

just a minute
請稍等一下，並且很快即回覆對方後續。

puts Mr. Robinson on hold
"put sb on hold" 請某人不掛斷電話等待。

you've been out of touch
"be out of touch"，失去聯繫；聯絡不上。

gesture
(v.) 做手勢示意、傳達某事。

wrapped up
"wrap up / wrap sth up"結束（某事）；完成（某事）。跟外國人開會，常會聽到這個說法表示會議到此結束。"a wrap-up"則指簡短的摘要或結論，意思與 summary 相同。

make something up

編造（故事、藉口）。

no dramas

= no worries，沒關係。drama 為戲劇之意，一個人如果很戲劇化，就很容易發生很多的紛亂、麻煩，因此 drama 可引申為讓人激動或焦慮的狀況、小插曲。"drama queen" 就用來指「小題大作的人」，表示遇到一點小事，就反應很大。

chock-a-block

爆滿；塞滿的意思。"be chock-a-block with sth" 就是充滿某物的意思。

be in touch with you

跟某人聯繫（通常指透過電話或信件）。

Finding a suitable candidate for a new position

替新職缺找合適的人選

Howard and Wesley are on a conference call with Jo, a head hunter from Indonesia, who is recommending some possible candidates for an upcoming position. Jo is speaking a little fast during the **con call.**

浩爾和衛斯理正在和印尼獵才公司的喬進行電話會議。喬正在為新開的職位推薦幾位人選，**電話會議**中，他的語速有點快。

Jo： There's Rajesh from Delhi, who's a real straight shooter. **No messing around with him.** Then Ahmedi-Al Amaar from Saudi Arabia. He's really on the ball. Finally, there's Hudali from Nepal and she's **a great ace to have up your sleeve**.

喬： 拉傑什來自德里，為人誠實、說話直接，跟他共事**不能打馬虎眼**。接下來是沙烏地阿拉伯的阿梅帝·阿馬，反應快又機警。最後是來自尼泊爾的胡達里，是個**傑出的人才**。

Wesley：	Wait, hold on a sec.
衛斯理：	等等，稍等一下。
Howard：	**Let's rewind.** Can I just stop you there, Jo? Would you mind repeating those candidates, please?
浩爾：	**回到剛剛說的部份**。喬，麻煩先暫停一下。可以請你重複一次這些人選的名字嗎？

Wesley：	Yes, who is the second candidate and how do we spell that name correctly?
衛斯理：	是啊，第二個人是誰？他的名字怎麼拼呢？
Jo：	Do you have a pen?

喬： 你有筆嗎？

Howard： **Yep!**

浩爾： **當然有。**

Jo： Ahmedi-Al Amaar is a **solid** choice from Saudi Arabia with **buckets of** experience. That's A-H-M-E-D-I dash A-L space A-M-A-A-R.

喬： 阿梅帝・阿馬是個**不錯**的選擇，他來自沙烏地阿拉伯且擁有**極豐富的**經驗。英文名字是 A-H-M-E-D-I，破折號，A-L，空格，A-M-A-A-R。

Howard： Great, thanks. The final candidate is Nepalese, right? The candidates are Indian, Saudi Arabian and Nepalese respectively, yeah?

浩爾： 太好了，謝謝。最後一位人選是尼泊爾人，對吧？這三個人各來自印度、沙烏地阿拉伯及尼泊爾，資訊都正確嗎？

Jo： Exactly, yes! The final one I mentioned is Hudali that's H-U-D-A-L-I.

喬： 正是，完全沒錯。最後一位人選胡達里，名字拼法是 H-U-D-A-L-I。

Wesley： Jo, let's leave it there for today. Howard and I, need to **mull it over** with Dean and HR.

衛斯理： 喬，今天就到此為止吧。浩爾和我需要再與迪恩及人資部**好好斟酌**一下。

Howard： Thanks for the effort Jo, we gotta **make tracks** as we have to catch a high speed train in an hour from main station.

浩爾： 喬，辛苦了。我們得**趕緊走了**，要趕在一小時內去總站搭高鐵。

Jo： Bye guys, safe travels.

喬： 回頭見，祝你們一路平安。

商英譯起來

con call

"conference call" 的縮略，電話會議。

straight shooter

剛正正直的人，說話不拐彎抹角、不說假話。

No messing around with him.

"mess around" 是指浪費時間做不重要的事；漫不經心地做某件事。本對話中的 " no messing around with sb" 指的是跟這個人做事不能馬虎的意思。

on the ball

專心、聰明、反應快的，也就是機靈、靈敏的意思。這個慣用語源自棒球，投手投球的速度或旋轉，可以讓打者三振出局。

a great ace to have up your sleeve

"have an ace up one's sleeve" 擁有王牌 (傑出人才) 的意思，也可以說 "have an ace in the hole"。

let's rewind

回到剛剛說的部份。rewind (v.) 是倒帶的意思，這個片語也就是指回到之前所說的內容。

yep

yeah、 yup、 yep 都是 yes「是的」的意思，也都是比較輕鬆的口語用法。

solid

形容物品有堅硬、實心的意思，引申為可靠的、牢靠的。

buckets of

大量的，相當於 "a lot of"。

mull it over

"mull over" 為好好考慮，仔細思考的意思。

make tracks

迅速離開某處。

Miscommunication on the phone
講電話的誤會

Dean and Howard are on a call to Dave who is having **a site visit** with a supplier located out of town.

迪恩與浩爾正在和戴夫通電話,戴夫正在**訪視**供應商位在郊區的廠房。

Dean： Dave, you are **obsessed** with this supplier recently. How is everything going with them?

迪恩： 戴夫,感覺你最近**很愛找這位廠商聯繫**,那邊進度如何?

Dave： I'm not **upset** with them! I think they are doing a great job. I just want to secure the new contract with them and make sure everything is running smoothly.

戴夫： 我和他們沒有相處**不快**啊!他們做得很好,我只是想要確保合約與進展順利。

Dean： No, I said **obsessed** not **upset**.

迪恩： 不，我是說「**愉快**」不是「**不快**」。

Dave： Ah okay, got it. The connection here isn't great. Yeah, the supplier is content with the progress so far. They will prepare the new contract today for signing but, I don't think we will get the increase we had hoped for.

戴夫： 哦，我懂了，這裡收訊不太好。是的，廠商對目前的進度很滿意，他們會準備好今天要簽的合約，但我覺得還達不到理想中的數字。

Howard： I guess **half a loaf is better than none.**

浩爾： 我覺得**有總比沒有來得好**。

Dave： True. **Hold on a sec** guys, their **CFO** is **hovering over.**

戴夫： 確實。**等一下**，各位，他們的**財務長在附近**。

The call goes silent and Dean and Howard can hear Dave mumbling in the background

*** 通話變安靜，迪恩和浩爾可以聽到另一邊的戴夫含糊不清的聲音 ***

Dean： Did he say UFO?

迪恩： 他是說「飛碟」嗎？

Howard： No, it was the CFO.

浩爾： 不是，是「財務長」。

Dean： I was wondering what that was, ha-ha.

迪恩： 哈哈，我還在想他在說什麼。

Dave： Okay guys, **to be pacific**, the CFO is not keen on increasing the amount this quarter but he **assures me** he will consider it for the next review meeting.

戴夫： 各位，「**平和**」來說，財務長在這一季不會太注重銷售數字。但他**保證**，這將會是下次審查會議的重點。

Howard： You mean **specific**, right? Well, I'm glad we **nipped it in the bud**, today!

浩爾：　你是要說「**具體**」對吧？嗯，我很開心這件事提前完成了，**防患於未然**。

Dave：　Did you say butt, Howard? I'm not sure if I heard that right?

戴夫：　你說「臀部」嗎？我聽不太清楚。

Howard：　Bud not butt ha-ha. A lot of people confuse those two words.

浩爾：　哈哈，是「防患未然」啦！真的有好多人會聽錯呢。

Dave：　No worries. I will speak to you guys tomorrow when I'm back in the office. I'm going to have dinner with the wife tonight. You know what they say; **happy wife, happy life**.

戴夫：　別擔心，我明早回辦公室時會再與你們詳談。今晚我得與老婆共進晚餐，你們知道的「**老婆開心，家庭就幸福**」嘛！

Dean：　Sure thing. Always good to have your priorities in order. See you tomorrow, Dave.

迪恩：　確實是這樣，把自己的優先順序排好順位才是聰明的作法。明天見，戴夫。

Dave：　Bye, guys.

戴夫：　回頭見，各位。

商英譯起來

a site visit

site (n.)（建築物的）地點，位置；（某事發生的）地點，現場。"a site visit"也就是去現場勘查的意思。

obsessed

(a.) 癡迷，著迷，心心念念的。

upset

(a.) 傷心；沮喪。

half a loaf is better than none

聊勝於無，有總比沒有好。

hold on a sec

請稍等一下，也常寫作 "just a sec"，sec = second 一秒鐘的意思。

CFO

= Chief Financial Officer，財務長。

hovering

hover (v.) 徘徊、靠近某人事物的意思。

pacific

和平的。本對話為口誤，應該是 "specific"。

assures me

assure (v.) 向……保證；使……放心。

specific

(a.) 明確的；具體的。對話中其實 Dave 真正要表達的是，"to be specific"，也就是嚴格來說的意思。

nipped it in the bud

"nip sth in the bud" 防患於未然。bud 是花蕾、芽的意思，而這整句是在敘述某件事情於萌芽狀態即被消滅。

happy wife, happy life

老婆舒心，生活開心。要享有幸福的生活，討好老婆大人就對了！

Presentations and Interactions

31

簡報及互動

35

39

Morning Huddle
晨會

Howard, Kate, and Dave are in an early Monday morning meeting. Mike, one of the head managers, is trying to motivate the others and determine their goals for the coming week.

浩爾、凱特、戴夫正參與週一早會。總經理麥可希望能激勵與會者，讓他們訂定未來一週的目標。

Mike： Thanks for joining our **huddle** so early everyone. I want to know how our latest project is doing. It looks like we've been **running out of steam** recently. What's the go?

麥可： 謝謝大家一早就來參與**會議**，我想知道我們最新的專案進展，最近似乎有些**缺乏動力**，現在進展如何呢？

Kate： We've had to change our goals slightly as we have faced some difficult obstacles but **from my end**, I know we're willing to **go the extra mile** to make sure it gets back on track ASAP.

凱特： 我們現在正面臨一些困難，所以得稍微調整目標，不過**在我看來**，大家都自願**多花一些心力**來確保一切盡快回到正軌。

Mike： I hope so! We have to **eat, sleep, and breathe** this project for the next 3 weeks. Because, at the moment we're **at a standstill**. Dave, have you informed the engineers and IT staff of the new direction we are going in?

麥可： 我也希望如此，未來三週我們必須**以這個專案為重**，因為目前我們處於**停滯期**。戴夫，你把我們的新方向告知工程師和 IT 人員了嗎？

Dave： I have, Mike, it has taken a while for them to **adapt** but they are **getting the hang of it**.

戴夫： 有的，麥可，他們花了不少時間**適應**，快要**抓到訣竅**了。

Howard： I have also been in touch with our suppliers, it looks as if the stock may **devaluate** slightly but it shouldn't **cause too much of a stir** for us. I think we have found solutions to our challenges.

浩爾： 我跟供應商有密切聯絡，看來庫存可能會稍微**貶值**，不過對我們應該不會**造成太多影響**。我覺得我們已經找到應對方法了。

Mike： Good to hear. Well, I think you all know what you need to do for today and for this coming week. Before I head off to San Francisco, I've got time for a quick coffee. You all keen? I'm hardly going to ask you to boost our performance and sales without a good cup of coffee. Let's be realistic!

麥可： 真是太好了，我想各位已經知道今天和未來一週該做些什麼了。在我去舊金山之前，還有空喝個咖啡，各位有興趣嗎？我想要求各位提升員工表現和業績，但沒請大家先喝個咖啡實在說不過去，我們還是現實一點。

Dave：	Thank God for that. You read my mind, Mike.
戴夫：	謝天謝地，麥可你懂我。
Kate & Howard：	Sounds good!
凱特和浩爾：	聽起來很棒！
Mike：	Sweet. Let's walk n' talk...
麥可：	太好了，我們邊走邊講吧……

商英譯起來

huddle

(n.) 集合。美式足球隊員會聚集成一圈，聽下一輪比賽的戰術。也有秘密會議的意思，通常這樣的會議是小型的、臨時的，人數也不會太多。

running out of steam

失去動力。steam 是蒸氣，"run out of..." 是「用完……」的意思。如同一台機器的蒸氣如果用完了，就沒辦法運行。

from my end

從我負責工作的這端來說。也可寫成 "at my end"。

go the extra mile

多付出一些代價和努力，甚至超越該做的。

eat, sleep, and breathe this project

"eat, sleep, and breathe sth" 字面上為吃東西、睡覺及呼吸都離不開這件事。用來指很熱愛某事物，生活中不能沒有它的意思。

at a standstill

standstill（n.）停滯；停止，"at a standstill" 處於停滯狀態。單 still 一個字，是仍舊處在某個狀態，如果加上了動詞，如 "sit still"，就是坐好不動，"stand still" 則是原地站好之意，standstill 這邊做名詞使用，表示停滯在那個狀態不移動。

adapt

(v.) 適應。

getting the hang of it

"get the hang of it" 指學會做某件事，也就是抓到訣竅的意思。

devaluate

(v.) 使……貶值。value = 價值，evaluate = 評估其價值，字首 de- 有相反、減少的意思。

cause too much of a stir

stir (n.) 是攪拌的動作，"cause a stir" 是指引起騷動、麻煩的意思。

A briefing
簡報

Dean, Howard, Wesley, and Dave have come together for a briefing to ensure they are all on the same page for their recent project.

迪恩、浩爾、衛斯理以及戴夫一同參與簡報會議，以確定他們四位對近期的專案想法一致。

Dean : The shareholders have **cast doubt on** whether we can finish our CellX project on time and within budget. Let's prove them wrong!

迪恩： 對於我們是否能如期完成 CellX 專案，並控制在預算內，股東們**有些懷疑**，我們來證明我們做得到吧！

Wesley : Yes, exactly. Guys, **cast your mind back** to when we used to do this effortlessly. I'm on top of communication with media this week.

衛斯理： 說得對，各位**回想一下**，以前這對我們來說根本小

意思，我這週會**把握好**跟媒體的溝通。

Howard： A lot has changed since we joined this company. It's **morphed into** a **cut throat** industry but I believe we can get it done by the deadline date.

浩爾： 自從我們加入這家公司以來，很多事情都變了，產業**演變至今**，**競爭白熱化**，但我相信我們還是能在期限前完成的。

Dave： I've **squared off** all my tasks so, perhaps I can **give** one of you **a dig out**?

戴夫： 我這邊份內的工作都**搞定**了，所以也許我可以**支援**你們其中一人？

Dean： I need some help convincing Fred in Marketing. Do you think you can **work your charm** Dave?

迪恩： 我需要有人幫我說服行銷部的弗萊德，戴夫你覺的你的**個人魅力**能說服他嗎？

Dave： Leave it with me. He's **a tough nut to crack**.

戴夫： 就交給我吧，他真的**不是很好溝通**。

Howard： Wesley, have you spoken to Kate about the recent changes in the timeline? She told me yesterday she's on track for a Thursday **reveal**, but it actually has been **pushed back** until Friday.

浩爾： 衛斯理，你跟凱特提過時間表最近的更動了嗎？凱特昨天跟我說她在處理周四的**揭示**，但實際上，那件事已經**延到**週五了。

Wesley： Actually, no I haven't yet. Let me text her real quick while I remember it. I find lately, that if I don't do something immediately then I tend to forget about it. I just can't seem to focus these days.

衛斯理： 其實我還沒跟她說。趁現在還記得，我馬上傳訊息給她。我最近發現，事情不馬上做，我一下就會忘記，感覺最近自己很難專注。

Dave ： Try to **ease up on** the coffee and get some rest.

戴夫 ： **少喝點**咖啡，然後好好放鬆休息一下吧。

Wesley ： Good call, alright, let's get back to it. Chat to you at lunch!

衛斯理 ： 好主意，那我們晚點再討論吧，午餐見！

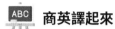 **商英譯起來**

cast doubt on...

"cast doubt on sth" 對某事懷有疑慮、表示懷疑。

cast your mind back

回想，追憶。

morphed into

"morph into"，轉變成⋯⋯。

cut-throat

(a.) 激烈的，殘酷無情的，"cut-throat competition" 就是指我們在商場上常用到的割喉戰。

squared off

"square off"，搞定。也可用於擺好架勢，準備迎戰。

give...a dig out

「幫⋯⋯找出生路；幫忙」。原意指把別人從深淵裡挖出、救出，也可說 "give a hand to"。

work your charm

發揮你的魅力。

a tough nut to crack

棘手的事物；難搞的人。

push back

拖遲；推遲。delay 或 postpon 皆有相似的意思。

ease up on...

「減少使用……」的意思，如 "My doctor told me to ease up on the smoking."。

Talking shop with the new GM
跟總經理談公事

Dean and Howard are talking with Jack, the newly appointed General Manager (GM) and giving him an update on the local market.

迪恩和浩爾正在和新上任的總經理傑克聊天，並向他報告本地市場的最新狀況。

Jack： It's great to finally meet you both in person! So, tell me guys, what's the market like here? Can we succeed and increase our profit margin? Tell me all about our customer base. Wesley gave me **the lowdown** but, I'm looking for some more **depth** from you both.

傑克： 終於見到你們本人真是太好了！可以跟我說明一下這邊的市場狀況嗎？我們能成功增加我們的利潤嗎？給我有關客戶群的全部資訊，衛斯理已跟我說一些**重要資訊**了，不過我想從你們兩位再多了解一些**細節**。

Dean： Well Jack, things have been a little quiet since we had the **Mid-Autumn festival** here and then there was the **bank holiday** weekend in the UK and Ireland which meant sales were low compared to this exact time last year.

迪恩： 傑克，**中秋節**後，是英國跟愛爾蘭的**國定假日**，所以近期銷售表現平平，銷售額較去年同期低。

Jack： I see. So, what was our net profit margin in **Q1** and **Q2**?

傑克： 我瞭解了。那麼，我們**第一季**和**第二季**的銷售淨利是多少呢？

Howard： It was $3.4 million, which is a 4% increase. Not entirely amazing but, **nothing to be sniffed at** either!

浩爾： 340 萬，較以往成長了 4%。數字不是特別驚人，不過也表現得**可圈可點**了。

Dean： As Howard mentioned, we had a small increase in Q1 and Q2 but at least we surpassed our **break-even point** substantially. Q3 and Q4 will be **tricky** going into Christmas and Chinese New Year.

迪恩： 就像浩爾說的，我們在第一季和第二季只有微幅成長，不過我們至少有大幅超過**損益平衡點**。在接下來的第三季和第四季，因為將碰上聖誕節和農曆新年，也會有些**棘手**。

Howard： True. The Government is planning to increase a **levy** they **enacted** last year. That may impact us locally. In order to maintain our growth, we may have **to contract out** some of our **in-house** operations to Vtex.

浩爾： 沒錯，政府正規劃增加他們去年**實施**的**稅收**，這對我們會有直接影響。為了維持成長，可能要考慮把我們的一些**內部**工作**外包**給 Vtex 公司。

Jack： I wouldn't worry too much about the Government. They're **a barking dog that seldom bites**. Besides, they have their own **geopolitical headaches** to worry about. Anyway, good to **touch base with** you two. Let's meet again towards the end of the week.

傑克： 我倒不太擔心政府那邊，那些政策大多都只是**虛張聲勢**而已，況且他們自己還有其他更**頭痛的事**。無論如何，很開心今天和你們**談談**，我們週末再見。

Dean： Sure, that's a good idea!

迪恩： 當然，沒問題！

商英譯起來

the lowdown
真相，實情，重要資訊。

depth
(n.) 深度。

Mid-Autumn Festival
中秋節。fall 和 autumn 兩個字皆可用來當作秋天的意思。

bank holiday
公定假日。指的是英國銀行和大部份企業不用上班的假期。

Q1 and Q2
第一季，第二季。一年有四季，quarter 這個字為四分之一，商業用語也就將 Q1~Q4 訂為四季訂定目標時的縮寫。

nothing to be sniffed at
不可小覷；值得認真對待。sniff 有嗤之以鼻、輕蔑地說的意思。而 "nothing to be sniffed at" 則是得慎重對待的意思。也可寫作 "not to be sniffed at"。

break-even point
損益平衡點。

tricky
(a.) 棘手，不好解決。

levy
(n.) 徵收的稅款。

enacted
enact (v.)，實施 (尤指法律上的)，立法。

contract out...
把……對外發包。

in-house
(a.) 在組織或機構內部的。

a barking dog that seldom bites
會叫的狗不會咬人，虛張聲勢。

geopolitical headaches
地緣的麻煩。

touch base with
跟某人溝通了解他們的想法。

Week 30

Handling queries during a presentation
簡報期間回答問題

Dave is in India, giving a presentation to Rajish and Agash, two experienced suppliers. He hopes to **secure** their business but is feeling nervous and deals with some **turbulent** situations effectively.

戴夫在印度，向兩位資深供應商—拉杰什和阿加什發表簡報。戴夫希望能談成他們的生意，但是心裡有點緊張，還要有效地處理一些**騷動**。

Dave： As you can see our growth has **skyrocketed** in the last two years and our future is looking **promising**.

戴夫： 如您所視，我們近兩年的成長**突飛猛進**，前景也十分看好。

- -

Agash： Excuse me, Dave. But what happened last year when the company was involved with that

'Copygate' scandal?

阿加什： 不好意思，戴夫，去年貴公司捲進**「抄襲門」醜案**
是怎麼回事？

Dave： That's a good question you raised, Agash but,
I'd appreciate if we could **leave all queries**
until the end of the presentation. I have some
essential material I'd love for you both to see.

戴夫： 這是個好問題，不過阿加什，**如果這個疑慮可以留**
待簡報結束後再來討論，我會很感謝。我還有其他
重要資料想給兩位過目。

Agash： Ok, but I'd like to know more at the end how you **weathered that storm**. I don't want our company associated with negative **publicity**.

阿加什： 好，不過在簡報結束後，我想聽你談談你們公司當初是如何**度過那風暴**的。我不希望我們公司有任何負面**形象**。

Dave： I completely understand. We have **made leaps and bounds** since that **hiccup**. I can address it more closely later on. Moving onto the next slide, it is evident we are on the right track going f- (Agash interrupts Dave.)

戴夫： 我完全瞭解。我們公司在那個**小插曲**之後**突飛猛進**，待會兒我會再仔細**談談**。接下來我們看到下一張投影片，很明顯地，我們目前正往對的方向發……(阿加什打斷了戴夫)

Agash： Mr. Dave, how many units will you commit to taking from us if we decide to work with you?

阿加什： 戴夫先生，如果我們決定和貴公司合作，你們承諾會從我們這訂購多少元件呢？

Dave： Our **consignment** figure will depend closely on our output expectations. As I mentioned before, let me explain more in detail when I wrap up what I have covered.

戴夫： 我們的**寄售**量和預期產量密切相關，而如同我前面所說的，待我總結報告內容的時候會再詳細說明。

Agash： Hmmm, okay. I like to **call a spade a spade** so excuse my bluntness, Dave.

阿加什： 恩，好，我這個人喜歡**有話直說**，戴夫不好意思。

Dave： We would love to cooperate and do business with you as we feel we can really make **inroads** into this area of the sector. Let's take a closer look at the market potential which we are dealing with. This information can be found on the next page of the handouts I gave you both.

戴夫： 我們很希望能和貴公司合作，也相信我們能在市場**有一番作為**。接著，我們來詳細看看目前市場潛力如何，講義的下一頁有相關資訊。

商英譯起來

turbulent

(n.) 騷動；混亂。turbulence 也可以用來指飛機遇到的亂流。

skyrocketed

skyrocket (v.) 暴漲；衝上雲霄。

promising

(a.) 有前途的；有出息的。

"copygate" scandal

"copygate" 這個字是 copy + -gate（一門），"-gate" 這個詞根是從 watergate 而來，而 scandal 是醜聞的意思。"copygate scandal" 是指抄襲醜聞。

*"watergate scandal" 水門事件的緣由。1972 年 6 月 17 日晚上，五名歹徒潛入水門大廈的民主黨辦公室安裝竊聽器遭到逮捕，當時的美國總統尼克森以及其內閣試圖掩蓋事件真相，FBI 在其中一名歹徒帳戶發現一筆來自尼克森連任委員會的匯款，竊聽陰謀終被發現，但尼克森依舊阻撓國會調查，最終導致憲政危機，尼克森於 1974 年宣布辭去美國總統職務。自此凡是有關美國的政治醜聞都冠以「一門」(-gate)。

I'd appreciate if...

"I would appreciate if..."，「如果可以⋯⋯我會不勝感激（用於禮貌的請求）」。

leave all the queries until the end of the presentation

"leave...until..."，「等到⋯⋯再去⋯⋯」。整句就是等到簡報後再來討論你們的疑慮。

weathered that storm

"weather the storm",走過風暴;度過難關。

publicity

(n.) 宣傳;推廣。

made leaps and bounds

"make leaps and bounds",突飛猛進。

hiccup

(n.) (造成短暫延誤或中斷的) 小問題。hiccup 其實是打嗝的意思,講話中間如果打嗝,即會中斷談話,故引申為打斷流程的小問題。

consignment

(n.) 託運的貨物。

call a spade a spade

直言不諱,實話實說。

make inroads

取得進展。

Visiting the doctor while on a business trip
出差時看醫生

Dave is visiting the doctor while on a business trip in India. He doesn't feel well and fears it may be something serious.

戴夫在印度出差時去看醫生，他身體不太舒服並擔心症狀可能很嚴重。

Doctor： Please sit, what's the matter?

醫生： 請坐，身體哪裡不舒服？

Dave： I don't feel well. My stomach is sore and I can't stop going to the toilet. I feel very hot and cold at times. It's strange because I was **full of beans** when I arrived in Mumbai two days ago.

戴夫： 我覺得很不舒服，我的胃很痛，一直跑廁所，而且身體忽冷忽熱。奇怪的是前兩天剛到孟買的時候，**我精神還好好**的。

Doctor： Did you drink the tap water or have some bad food?

醫生： 你有喝自來水或吃了什麼怪東西嗎？

Dave： I'm not sure, we had a party after our conference and I can't **recall** because I had too many cocktails. I doubt my hotel would serve bad food, I mean, it's a four star hotel so I'd imagine that it should be ok!

戴夫： 我不太確定，我們會議結束後開了個派對，因為那時喝了太多雞尾酒，所以其他的我**回想**不起來了。我待的飯店不太可能有不潔的食物，我的意思是，畢竟那是間四星級飯店，我想它的食物應該沒問題才對。

Doctor： Mr. Dave Sir, you can get sick from the **unlikeliest** of places. Let's try **getting you back into shape**, ok?

醫生： 戴夫先生，有時都是**最想不到**的地方讓人生病，我們來想辦法讓你**恢復健康**，好嗎？

Dave： That'd be great **Doc** ; I just **can't keep anything down**.

戴夫： 拜託你了**醫生**，我最近**吃什麼都吐**。

Doctor： Don't worry; you won't be **kicking the bucket** anytime soon. It looks like you have **a bad case** of food poisoning and a fever, no **infection**. I'll prescribe some medicine for you. Are you **allergic** to anything?

醫生： 別擔心，這種小病**死**不了的。看來你有**嚴重的**食物中毒和發燒**症狀**，但沒有**感染**。我會開些藥給你，你有對什麼**過敏**嗎？

Dave： Allergic? What do you mean?

戴夫： 過敏？你指什麼？

Doctor： Do you **have** any **allergies to** certain medication or food? Penicillin, for example?

醫生： 你有**對**任何食物或藥物**過敏**嗎？例如有沒有對青黴素過敏？

Dave： No, I don't think so.

戴夫： 我想我都沒有。

- -

Doctor： Ok, I want to give you **an injection** to help with the vomiting and diarrhea. And I'll give you some tablets to take three times a day. Remember; drink plenty of water and rest. No alcohol for 7 days. That should **get you back on track**.

醫生： 好，那我幫你**打針**緩解嘔吐跟腹瀉，另外我也會開一些藥給你，一天服用三次。切記要多喝水跟休息，然後至少七天不能喝酒，這樣**身體應該會好很多**。

Dave： Perfect, thanks Doc.

戴夫： 太好了，謝謝醫生。

商英譯起來

was full of beans

"be full of beans" 活力十足,精力充沛。

recall

(v.) 聯想,回憶起。

unlikeliest

unlikely (adj.) 不是你想像的;不太可能發生的。unlikeliest 是 unlikely 的最高級, 代表最不可能發生的事情。

getting you back into shape

" get sb back into shape" 讓某人恢復健康。shape 有情況及健康狀況的意思, "keep in shape" 及 "stay in shape" 都是指保持健康的意思。 "in good shape" 則是指健康;而 "in bad shape" 或 "out of shape" 則是不太健康的意思!

Doc

doctor 的縮寫,也就是稱呼醫生的口語用法。

can't keep anything down

"keep sth down" 能吃 / 喝下東西而不吐。

kicking the bucket

"kick the bucket",翹辮子;死掉。bucket 在古字裡面有房子裡的「樑」之意。古時的農家在宰殺畜生時,會把繩子綁在牠們的腳上,然後把牠們掛在大樑上。動物會做垂死的掙扎,腳不停的踢那根大樑,這就是這個片語的由來,與中文會用的 `「掛了」意思相近。不過要注意的是,這句俗語不宜用在討論長輩或尊敬的對象過世。

a bad case

嚴重的病例。

infection

(n.) (由細菌或病毒造成的) 感染。

are you allergic to...

"be allergic to...",對……過敏。

injection

(n.) 打針。

get you back on track

重回軌道,重振旗鼓。重返本來被中斷的工作或任務繼續打拼。

Workplace ethics and behaviour
職場倫理及舉止

Dave, Howard and Ben (a member of the staff) are having a heated discussion about Ben's performance and his behaviour in work. It appears Ben is somewhat of a bully. Tempers get a little out of control.

戴夫、浩爾、班（其中一名職員）正激烈討論著班的業績和工作表現。班似乎十分霸道，雙方的情緒都開始有些失控。

Howard： So, you're telling me that your productivity has been **stellar** recently? **I wasn't born yesterday** you piece of sh-...

浩爾： 所以你的意思是你最近業績很**亮眼**？**別把我當三歲小孩耍**！你這垃……

Dave： Let's just all **take a chill pill**, all right? Ben, we're not happy with how you conduct yourself in the office and how you've been treating your co-workers. Michelle told us you took a picture of her while she was bending over the photocopier. I mean this is just unacceptable. What were you thinking?

戴夫： 我們大家都**冷靜一點**，好嗎？班，我們對你在辦公室的表現以及對待同事的方式很不滿意。米雪兒跟我們說，你趁她彎腰影印東西的時候偷拍她，這樣的行為真的不能接受，你腦袋到底在想什麼？

Ben： I didn't think it w-...

班： 我不覺得有什……

Howard： **I for one** will not stand for that sort of behaviour. It's disgusting. I'm not saying this just because I'm **hangry**. I really mean It, Ben.

浩爾： **我個人**完全無法忍受那種行為，簡直噁心至極，我不是因為**又餓又氣**才這樣說，我是認真的，班。

Dave： Let's keep it down guys. I think Frank is **floating around** the office. If he **gets wind of** this we may **be in deep water**.

戴夫： 各位小聲一點，我覺得法蘭克就**在辦公室附近**，如果他**聽到**的話，我們可能都要**倒大楣**了。

Ben： Guys, I just want to say I never meant to offend anyone. I told you both after I got my first warning that I could **turn over a new leaf** and I feel like I...

班： 各位，我只想說，我從來沒有想侵犯任何人，我從第一次被警告後就跟你們說了，我希望能**改過自新**，我覺得我⋯⋯

Howard： I honestly don't think you have. We can't be **implicated** in another **#Metoo movement**. I don't want our reputation destroyed at the expense of some **Alpha dick** who thinks his actions won't have consequences.

浩爾： 我認真不覺得你會有什麼改變，我們可不能跟 **#Metoo 運動**扯上任何關係，我不希望我們公司的名聲因為一個做事不想後果的**混蛋**而毀於一旦。

商英譯起來

somewhat of a bully

"somewhat of + N"，「有點……」，somewhat 後面也可以直接加形容詞，如："somewhat tired"有點累。

stellar

(a.) 傑出的；優秀的。

I wasn't born yesterday

別把我當三歲小孩耍；我不是傻子。

take a chill pill

吃一片冷靜的藥片，意指冷靜一點，與 "calm down" 同意。

I for one...

我個人……（用在表達自己的意見，儘管他人可能有其他想法）。

hangry

此為 hungry 和 angry 二字合併所產生的新字彙。意為又餓又氣。

floating around

" float around"（雖然沒看到但感覺）就在附近。

gets wind of ...

聽到……的風聲，得到……消息。

be in deep water

陷入困境；惹上麻煩。

turn over a new leaf

改過自新。這裡的 leaf 其實代表書的頁面，也就是我們常用的 page，翻了新的一頁，代表著生活會有個新的開始。

implicated

implicate (v.) 牽連；涉及。

#Metoo moment

「#MeToo」是 2017 年 10 月哈維‧韋恩斯坦性騷擾事件後在社交媒體上廣泛傳播的一個主題標籤，用於譴責性侵犯與性騷擾行為。「#MeToo」這個用語在社群媒體上面廣泛的被使用和傳播，也用以鼓勵人們在社群媒體上公開自己的不愉悅經歷，使人們能認識到這些行為的嚴重性。

alpha dick

頭號渾蛋。alpha (a.) 用在名詞前，指一群人中「領頭的，最有影響力的」。

Firing an employee
解雇員工

Ben has committed another inappropriate offence by taking up skirt pictures of his female colleagues and sending them to other coworkers. This, is therefore the final straw for him as he has been called into a meeting with HR. Chloe from HR is with Ben. In attendance are Wesley and Tim, a member of the labour union. The tone of the meeting is somewhat subdued.

班又重操惡習,他偷拍女同事的**裙底風光**,還傳給其他同事。這樣的行為成為了**壓倒駱駝的最後一根稻草**,班被叫到人資部開會,人資部的克柔伊陪同班一起,出席會議的還有衛斯理和工會的提姆,整場會議很**安靜**。

Chloe： Ben, thanks for joining us today. I'm not going **to beat around the bush**. I'd like to discuss your recent **blunder**. Quite frankly it is completely unacceptable and illegal. It is evident that we have given you multiple warnings **in accordance**

with the national labour regulations.

克柔伊： 班，謝謝你今天來參加會議，我也就不**拐彎抹角**了，我想和你談談你最近的**不當的行為**。坦白說，你的所作所為讓人無法接受而且已經違法，我們之前也**以勞工法**多次警告過你。

Tim： At this stage Ben, I must **concur** with Chloe's statement. You **violated** two labour regulations **in accordance with** the laws. I must warn you that this will result in **termination** from this company. Do you have anything to say for yourself?

提姆： 班，都到了這個階段，我只能**同意**克柔伊的說法了。**根據**法律，你**違反**了兩項勞工法，我必須警告你這些行為將導致被公司**解僱**，你還有什麼要說的嗎？

Ben： I do yes! Firstly, I would like to sincerely apologize for my actions. I understand that it **got out of hand**.

班： 我有！首先，我想為我的行為道歉，我知道那樣的行為已經**失控**了。

Wesley： What the hell were you thinking?

衛斯理： 你腦袋到底裝什麼？

Ben： I wasn't.

班： 我那時沒多想……

Wesley： Clearly!

衛斯理： 不用說也知道。

Chloe： As Tim mentioned, we will be terminating your contract **as of** today. We would ask you to collect all your personal belongings and follow security who are waiting outside the room for you. We will be in touch regarding your final pay and **particulars**.

克柔伊： 就像提姆所說的，我們**今天起**就會終止與你的合約。請收拾好你所有的個人物品，並跟著等在外頭的保全人員走，我們會再跟你聯絡，告知你最後一期的薪資和相關**細節**。

Wesley： Allow me **to show you to the door**.

衛斯理： 我**送你出去**吧。

***Ben gets up and leaves the meeting room. There is silence. ***
班站起來並離開會議室，現場一片安靜。

Chloe： Well I'm glad that's behind us. He **gave me the creeps**!

克柔伊： 我很開心一切總算過去了，那傢伙真的讓我**渾身起雞皮疙瘩**。

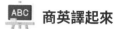 **商英譯起來**

up skirt pictures
裙底風光的照片 (通常為被偷拍的)。

the final straw
或 "the last straw" 壓垮駱駝的最後一根稻草。

in attendance
出席；與會。

subdued
小聲的；悶悶不樂的；(光線) 昏暗的。

beat around the bush
拐彎抹角。

blunder
(n.) 犯的錯。

in accordance with
依據 (法條)；依 (要求)。

concur
(v.) 同意。等同 agree。

violated
violate (v.) 違反 (通常嚴重性較大，比如法律層面相關)。

termination

(n.) 終止 (通常指協議或合約)。

got out of hand

"get out of hand"，失控。

as of...

自……起。

particulars

(n.) 細節，等同 details.

show you to the door

下逐客令。如果是禮貌的送客，可以用 "I will walk you out."。

give me the creeps

讓我覺得不自在，"give sb the creeps" 不舒服，令人毛骨悚然。

Week 34

Networking at a seminar
研討會中建立人脈

Wesley **has been tasked with** the responsibility of representing the company at the upcoming Global Techchain Summit. His mission is to **network** and promote the company whilst learning from industry leaders. During the **intermission** he decides **to have a ramble** and begins to **mingle with** the other professionals.

衛斯理**被指派**代表公司參加即將到來的全球技術高峰會。他的任務是**建立人脈**、推廣公司，並向其他產業領袖學習。**中場休息**時，他決定去找人**閒聊**，並多和其他專業人士**互動**。

*** Wesley catches the eye of a person as he digs into the refreshments on offer***
在享用會場提供的餐點時，衛斯理和另一個人對到眼

Wesley： **I take it** you're not just here for the prawn cocktail and cheese plates?

衛斯理： **我想**你今天來這，不是只為了雞尾酒蝦沙拉跟起司拼盤吧？

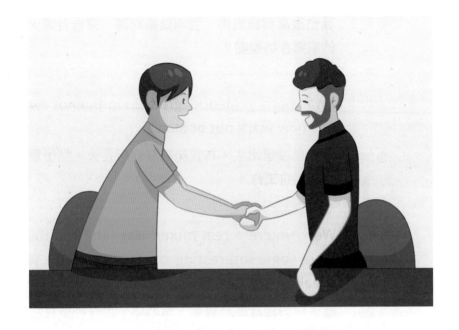

New Person： I've been here 5 years running so I guess you could say I am ha-ha. Nice to meet you, I'm Barry.

新朋友： 我已經連續參加這個活動五年了，所以你可以當我單純來吃東西而已，哈哈。很高興認識你，我叫貝瑞。

Both men shake hands accordingly
兩人握手

Wesley： **The feeling's mutual.** I'm Wesley from Taiwan. Where abouts do you **hail from**?

衛斯理： **我也很高興認識你**，我叫做衛斯理，來自台灣，你的**家鄉在哪裡呢**？

Barry： I was born in Madrid, grew up in Buenos Aires and now **work out of** Manila.

貝瑞： 我在馬德里出生，布宜諾斯艾利斯長大，然後現在在馬尼拉**工作**。

Wesley： Wow, you're a real **mixed bag**, eh? You must have some interesting stories to tell. Do you speak Spanish?

衛斯理： 哇，你的**經歷**還真**豐富**，想必你一定有許多有趣的故事吧，你會說西班牙語嗎？

Barry： **Si Senor!** I've been told I have many **feathers in my cap** but I don't like **to brag**. Tell me Wesley, what do you think of the seminar so far? Is this your first time here?

貝瑞： **會的，先生！**很多人都覺得我有許多**豐功偉業**，不過我不喜歡**吹噓**。衛斯理，你目前覺得這場研討會如何？你是第一次來參加嗎？

Wesley： Yes. My boss was due to come but he is on a business trip in Tokyo, so I**'ve been handed the reins**.

衛斯理： 對，我老闆本來要來，但他正在東京出差，所以**我才能被派來參加**。

Barry： Well, you know what they say, **fortune favours the bold!**

貝瑞： 你知道的，人們常說：「**勇者得助。**」

Wesley： That's very true. I hope to be **a keen traveller** like you one day. These business trips are new for me but I am embracing them. Here, please take my business card and let me know if we could have the chance to cooperate in the future.

衛斯理： 說得沒錯，我希望自己有朝一日也能像你一樣，**走遍大江南北**。像這樣來出差對我來說很新鮮，我正在習慣中，這是我的名片，未來若有機會合作的話歡迎聯絡我。

Barry： Perfect, will do. **Adios** Wesley!

貝瑞： 沒問題，**再見**了衛斯理！

商英譯起來

has been tasked with...

"be tasked with..." 被派給⋯⋯的任務。

network

(v.) (為了工作) 建立關係網，建立人脈。

intermission

(n.) (電影、戲劇、音樂會) 的中場休息時間。

have a ramble

（沒有特定目的的）閒聊；閒晃。

mingle with

（在社交場合）到處走動跟人說話。

refreshments

(n.) (派對或會議提供的) 小茶點、飲料。

I take it...

我猜想；我認為。

The feeling's mutual.

兩個人對對方有同樣的想法。所以當貝瑞說："Nice to meet you." 衛斯理回答："The feeling's mutual."（我也有同樣感受）就是表示「我也很高興認識你」的意思。

hail from
來自……; 出生於……。

work out of
在 (某個地點) 努力工作。

mixed bag
混合體, 大雜燴。

Si Senor
是的, 先生。(西語)

feathers in my cap
"a feather in one's cap" 引以為傲的成就。

brag
(v.) 自誇, 吹噓。

have been handed the reins
rein (n.) 是公司或組織的權限, 常用複數 "reins", "be handed the reins" 被賦予權限。

fortune favours the bold
天助自助者; 勇者得助 (文中寫的是英式的拼法 favour, 美式則常用 favor)。

a keen traveller
愛好, 熱衷旅遊之人 (文中寫的是英式的拼法 traveller, 美式則常用 traveler)。

adios
為西班牙語中的「再會」, 現在也普及化用於英語系國家中代表熱情的道再見, good-bye。

Week 35

Week 35
Tips for presentations
簡報訣竅

Kate is preparing for a presentation but she is feeling very nervous and has asked Howard and Dean for some tips.

凱特正在準備幾簡報,不過她非常緊張,所以向浩爾和迪恩請教一些小訣竅。

Kate： I just feel a little **out of my depth** with this presentation I have to give next week guys, any advice?

凱特： 我對我下週的報告有點**沒把握**,兩位有什麼建議嗎?

Howard： Well you **gotta** remember the **5P's! Proper Preparation Prevents Poor Performance.** What I mean by that is that you must prepare as much as possible. Practice it and anticipate difficult questions.

浩爾： 說到這怎**麼能錯過**簡報的 **5S—準備得宜就能避免不好的表現**。5S 的重點就是事前準備愈多愈好，勤加練習，並預測觀眾可能提問的艱難問題。

Dean： One thing I like to do is to not have any paper in my hand only the remote control. Otherwise, people will know that you are **shaking like a leaf**. Another good thing to do is start well, for example try to **break the ice** in any way you can. That'll **ease the tension**.

迪恩： 我個人的習慣則是：手上只拿簡報筆不拿小抄，不然，別人就知道你**很緊張**。另一個小技巧是「開個好頭」，例如盡你所能的**破冰**，那樣也能**緩解緊張**。

Howard： That's a good point! Also, make sure to make eye contact with your audience. That way it'll show you are **engaging**, which in turn will get people to stay off their mobile phones. You know what **millennials** are like these days ha-ha.

浩爾： 說得真好！另外，記得要跟觀眾保持眼神接觸，那樣不但能**展現**你的**魅力**，也能讓觀眾不要一直滑手機，你也知道現在的千禧世代總是機不離手，哈哈。

Dean： You have **to throw yourself into** this presentation and do your best. One thing I like to do is to have a stroll around the room or stage. That shows you are comfortable in you environment, even if you aren't. Remember, **fake it till you make it!**

迪恩： 你必須**全心投入**在這簡報中並盡力做到最好。我個人喜歡在房間內或講台上**來回走動**，這樣也會讓人覺得你神色自若，儘管內心有些焦慮，記住，**演久就像了**。

Howard： Another thing that drives me crazy is when people put too much information on the slides. It defeats the whole purpose of a presentation.

I mean, we can all read. So, keep the writing to a minimum on each slide. Focus on expanding the topics and not just reading it from the scree-...

浩爾： 還有一件事我不能忍受，就是在一頁投影片塞太多資訊，那樣完全違背了簡報的目的。要用看的我們自己看就好了啊，每張投影片的字愈少愈好，重點是延伸主題，而不是什麼都打在螢幕……

Kate： Thanks guys, but I'm sorry I gotta run. Can we **catch up** again later today?

凱特： 謝謝你們，不過抱歉我得離開了，我可以今天晚點**再跟你們討論**嗎？

Dean： Sure. Go for it!

迪恩： 當然沒問題，去吧！

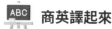 **商英譯起來**

out of my depth

不能勝任；無法駕馭。depth 是深度，這裡是說超過了自己可以負荷的深度，也就是有一種被淹沒的無助感。

gotta

我得要，就是" have got to"的簡略。

5P's! Proper Preparation Prevents Poor Performance.

簡報常見 5S，準備得宜就能避免不好的表現。

shaking like a leaf

"shake like a leaf"，一直在發抖。

break the ice

破冰，打破僵局。

engaging

(a.) 令人愉快；有吸引力的。

millennials

(n.) 千禧世代，泛指 1981 – 1996 年間出生的人，也可稱作 Y 世代（Generation Y）。另有 Generation X 代表 1965 – 1980 年間出生的人。

throw yourself into

全心投入。

stroll

(v.) 漫步；遊走；溜達。

fake it till you make it

演久了就像，假裝你是某人直到你成為某人。

catch up

(再) 相聚。

Tips for presentations 2
簡報訣竅 2

Kate is catching up with Dean and Howard in the office after work on how she can improve her presentation skills. She has ordered a round of pizzas for them all to share as a thank you gesture for their advice and input.

下班後，凱特繼續在辦公室與迪恩和浩爾討論如何提升簡報技巧。她為大家點了披薩一同享用，感謝他們給予意見和提點。

Kate： Thanks for meeting me guys. This presentation is my **Achilles' heel**. What other tips can you give me?

凱特： 謝謝兩位這麼晚還來陪我，這次的簡報真的是我的**罩門**，你們還有其他建議嗎？

Dean： Cheers for the pizza, Kate. I think a great thing to remember is to keep it a little shorter than the **allotted** time. That way you can give time to questions and answers. It also leaves your audience wanting more of you.

迪恩： 凱特，謝謝你的披薩。我覺得還要記得，盡量把時間控制得比**規定**時間還短，這樣問答才會有足夠的時間。縮短時間也會讓觀眾想聽你說更多。

Howard： I would also like to **reiterate** what Dean said that keeping the presentation short is essential. Have no more than 10 slides, speak for no more than 20 minutes and use font that is no bigger than size 30. They call it the 10-20-30 rule. It **works a treat** for me!

浩爾： 我也想**再次強調**，迪恩提到簡報要精簡，這點真的很重要。投影片不放超過 10 頁，不講超過 20 分鐘，投影片上的字體大小不超過 30。有人稱這為簡報的 10-20-30 定律。每次都**管用**。

Dean： I've also started implementing that rule and it's been pretty effective so far. For me, I like to tell short stories and give **cutting edge** examples that people can **relate to**. It helps you connect more effectively with your audience.

迪恩： 我也有實施這項技巧，到目前為止我覺得非常有效，我個人喜歡講小故事、並提供聽眾**最新穎**的例子，引起他們的**共鳴**，這樣能更有效地跟聽眾溝通。

Howard： Lastly, I guess the final piece of advice I can give you is to breathe. Take 5-10 minutes before you **are due to** give the presentation and go into a quiet room or bathroom and do slow, deep breathing. This may sound silly but actually it's a great way to help you think more clearly and **keeps those nerves at bay**.

浩爾： 最後還有一個小建議，那就是要調整呼吸，在你上臺報告前的 5 到 10 分鐘，先去廁所或安靜的房間深呼吸。這也許聽起來有點蠢，但對整理思緒和**不緊張**十分有效。

Kate： Wow! You guys are presentation masters. Much appreciated! I think I'm ready **to ace** this **baptism of fire**!

凱特： 哇！你們真是簡報大師，很感謝你們。我想我已經**摩拳擦掌、蓄勢待發**了！

商英譯起來

Achilles' heel

罩門、弱點、要害。源自希臘神話，Achilles（阿基里斯）的母親 Thetis 因為聽說冥河（Styx）之水可以使人變成刀槍不入，因此把兒子泡在冥河裡，但因為 Thetis 是抓著腳踝讓他泡在河裡的，因此漏掉了腳踝，阿基里斯之腱便成為他唯一的弱點，後來阿基里斯被劍射中腳踝而亡，典故由此而來。腳跟部位因為有條筋特別脆弱容易扭到，故也取名阿基里斯腱（Achilles' tendon）。

allotted

(a.) 分配的。

reiterate

(v.) 重申。

works a treat

"work a treat"，運作順利。

cutting edge

最先進的；領先位置。

relate to...

對……有共鳴。

are due to...

"be due to" 準備要……。

keeps those nerves at bay

"keep sth at bay" 阻止 (令人不快或危險的事物) 發生。

ace

(v.) 展現出一流的表現。

baptism of fire

初次的痛苦經驗,就如同士兵第一次上戰場。

Week 37

Working Overtime
加班

Dave's Boss has told him he needs to work overtime. Dave is feeling the pressure of the job and is discussing his schedule with Howard and Kate at the coffee dock.

戴夫的老闆要求他加班，戴夫對工作備感壓力，因此與浩爾和凱特在咖啡間討論工作行程。

Dave : I just don't see how we're going to get this project finished on time. The gaffer said he will pay me double for the overtime which is pretty fair, so I'm happy to do it because I need the money. I **haven't got two pennies to rub together** recently after buying the new Tesla.

戴夫： 我真的不覺得我們能在期限內完成專案，領班說我加班會付我雙倍薪水，這樣蠻合理的，我需要錢所以我欣然接受。最近我在買了特斯拉之後**捉襟見肘**。

Kate： Well, to be honest I don't think **the juice is worth the squeeze**.

凱特： 老實說，我不認為**那樣值得**。

Dave： Excuse me?

戴夫： 什麼意思？

Kate： I mean for the amount of effort and work that you're going to put in, I don't think it's worth **giving up** your weekend for. Do you know what I mean?

凱特： 我指的是你要投入大量心力在工作上，連週末都要**犧牲**在工作上不太值得吧，你懂我意思嗎？

Dave： Okay, I get it now. I hear what you're saying but I still think it's good because right now I could really do with the money. So, I will just do what **the puppet master** tells me to do.

戴夫： 好，我現在懂了，我理解你的意思，不過我目前還是覺得這樣比較好，至少我手頭不會那麼緊，所以**老闆**叫我做的事，我都會乖乖照辦。

Kate： **Each to their own.** But, I know what I would have done in your situation.

凱特： **大家都有選擇的權利**，不過換作是我，我絕對不會那樣。

Howard： I agree with Kate on this. You're working too much and don't have balance in your life. Anyway, **hang in there**, Dave! Have a good weekend.

浩爾： 這點我想法跟凱特一樣，你花太多時間在工作上了，生活會平衡，不過不管怎樣，**加油吧！**戴夫，週末愉快！

商英譯起來

haven't got two pennies to rub together

"not have two pennies to rub together" 口袋空空如也，連兩個能互相摩擦叮噹作響的錢幣都掏不出來，形容很窮困的意思。

the juice is worth the squeeze

值得付出的事。

giving up

"give up"，放棄。

the puppet master

雇主。puppet 是傀儡，這個詞原本是在講操縱傀儡賦予其生命的人，現在也可用在對某件事物有很大決定生殺大權的人身上，比如說老闆。

each to their own

"each to his/ her/ their own" 每個人各有所好。用來表示每個人都有不同的愛好。

hang in there

撐著點！

Week 38

Take a day off
放一天的假

Dean and Wesley bump into each other in the canteen. They had planned a presentation rehearsal with Howard, who is out sick today.

迪恩和衛斯理在員工餐廳遇到，他們原先預計要和浩爾一起排練簡報，不過浩爾今天請病假。

Wesley： Hey Dean, **what's the story?**

衛斯理： 嘿，迪恩，**發生什麼事？**

Dean： **Ah grand yeah!** Struggling with the new project. Have you heard from the **main man** today?

迪恩： **一個頭兩個大啊！**新專案難產中，你今天有見到我們的**主管**嗎？

Wesley： Howard? No, he's off today. He mentioned last night when he was getting into an Uber that he needed a day off today.

衛斯理： 你說浩爾嗎？沒耶，他今天請假，他昨晚搭上 Uber 時有提到他要請假。

Dean： **Slacking off** and up to his old **shenanigans** again? I didn't think you guys had that much to drink after I left? Were you both **plastered** ha-ha?

迪恩： 又再**耍花招偷懶**了嗎？哈哈，沒想到我走後你們喝那麼多，你們倆都**喝掛**囉？

Wesley： Actually, no we only had one more after you left. He said he needed a mental health day today, which is understandable.

衛斯理： 其實沒有，你走後我們只再喝了一杯。他說他需要放一天心理健康假，其實蠻能理解的。

Dean： For sure! He's **been snowed under** the last couple of weeks. I could do with a mental health day myself. It's great this company gives us days like that. It's so important to take care of our mental health.

迪恩： 那當然！浩爾最近幾週都**忙得不可開交**，我覺得我自己也需要一天的心理健康日了，公司願意給我們這樣的休假真的很棒，照顧心理健康的確很重要。

Wesley： I couldn't agree more. He deserves to **take his foot off the gas**. He's earned it. It's **once in a blue moon** that he takes a day off anyway.

衛斯理： 非常同意，他確實該**放鬆喘口氣了**，這是他應得的。他**難得**請假。

Dean： I guess we can leave that rehearsal until he's back in the office.

迪恩： 我想我們可以等他回來上班後再排練。

Wesley： Sure. Have you seen **the other fella**?

衛斯理： 當然，那你有看到**另一位仁兄**嗎？

Dean： Who, Dave? **Beats me!**

迪恩： 誰？你說戴夫嗎？**天曉得**。

 **商英譯起來**

what's the story
（問對方）發生什麼事？

ah grand yeah
頭大中。

the main man
最主要的人，在這裡可當主管或老闆使用。

slacking off
"slack off"，偷懶。

shenanigans
(n.) 把戲，詭計。

plastered
(a.) 爛醉的。也可以用 "very drunk" 或 "wasted" 代替。

he's been snowed under
"be snowed under"（因公務繁重）忙得不可開交。

to take his foot off the gas
把腳從油門上移開，有喘口氣，放鬆一下的意思。也可說 "take someone's foot off the pedal"。

once in a blue moon

非常罕見的。這個用語開始於 19 世紀初，根據專家的說法，火山爆發後或是茫茫大霧時，空氣中塵粒的大小與光的波長相同，因此人們肉眼所見的月亮便會呈現淺藍的顏色，然而這種景象發生的機率相當的低，也可以說千載難逢。

the other fella

另一位仁兄，fella 就是 fellow。

beats me

天曉得，不知道耶。就是就算你打我，我還是沒辦法說出來，因為我真的不知道。

Binge-watching a TV show
不分日夜地追劇

Dave and Kate are at the reception area discussing a recent TV show that has **caught the country by storm.**
戴夫和凱特在會客室討論最近**紅遍全國**的電視劇。

Kate： I saw this TV show on Netflix last night. It was so addictive; I started watching it at 7pm and finally **hit the hay** around 5am! It was **gripping**! Usually I **don't bat an eyelid** to some of the shows on it, but this one was brilliant.

凱特： 我昨晚在 Netflix 上看那部電視劇，真的很讓人上癮，我從晚上 7 點看到大概早上五點才**去睡**，真的很讓人**入迷**！我對電視劇都**無感**，但這部真的超推。

Dave： I don't think I've seen that one. What's the name of it?

戴夫： 我好像沒看過耶，那一部叫什麼？

Kate： Awh I can't remember the name it **was on the tip of my tongue** there but it's gone now, sorry. Actually, it is about this guy who'**s wrongfully convicted of** murder. Or so that's what we **are led to believe**. The **prosecutors** convince the jury and he is sent to life in prison. The rest I won't tell you.

凱特： 啊，我忘記劇名了，快想出來了**就在嘴邊**，但又想不起來了，不好意思。內容在講有個人被**誤判**謀殺，至少**目前大家是這樣想**。**檢察官**說服了陪審團，所以那人被判終身監禁，然後剩下的就不能說了。

Dave： Good! I hate **spoilers** ha-ha. So, how would you rate it?

戴夫： 好，我討厭別人**劇透**，哈哈，所以你對這部的評價如何？

Kate： I'd probably give it a 9. It's completely **bingeable**.

凱特： 我會給它 9 分吧，這部真的讓人**欲罷不能**。

Dave： That's pretty high. I don't have Netflix would you believe. Is it easy to get it set up?

戴夫： 給 9 分很高耶，不過你相信嗎，我還沒有 Netflix，安裝容易嗎？

Kate： Just register your details, provide your credit card number and you're **good to go**.

凱特： 只要註冊你的詳細資料、提供信用卡號碼，就**可以準備看了**。

Dave： **Spot on!** I'll give that a **look-see** tonight.

戴夫： **沒錯！**我今晚馬上就來**看看**。

ABC 商英譯起來

caught the country by storm

風靡了整個國家，"catch sb/sth by storm"，征服了……；在……爆紅。也可作 "take sb/ sth by storm"。

hit the hay

上床睡覺。以前西方社會的床是用乾草製成，躺上床拍打床鋪，延伸用為上床睡覺，也可以說 "hit the sack"。

gripping

(a.) 入迷；引人入勝的。

don't bat an eyelid

"not bat an eyelid/ eyelash"，不為所動。

was on the tip of my tongue

"be on the tip of one's tongue"，（想說的話）就在嘴邊。

was wrongfully convicted of

"be wrongfully convicted of..."，誤判成定……罪。

are led to believe

"lead sb to believe" 為「讓某人相信」的意思。這裡用被動式，被引導這樣相信著。

prosecutors

prosecutor (n.)，檢察官。

spoilers

spoiler (n.)，劇透，破梗（用於劇本影視上面居多）。

bingeable

binge (n.) 無節制的狂熱行為，如："a drinking binge"（狂飲）或 "an eating binge"（暴食）。bingeable (a.) 指容易上癮會被吸進去的活動。

are good to go

"be good to go"（準備好）進行活動。

spot on

(a.) 沒錯，= exactly right。

look-see

(n.) 掃一眼，看一下。

Written Communication

書信溝通

Reading post-it notes
閱讀便條

Dave has found some post-it notes on his desk from a colleague but he's having trouble understanding what they mean. He asks Sarah and Wesley if they have any idea.

戴夫在桌上發現一些同事寫給他的便條，但是他卻看不懂，於是他向莎拉和衛斯理尋求幫助。

Dave： Do you both know what these say, I can't **wrap my head around** them?

戴夫： 你們倆看的出來這些便條在寫什麼嗎？我完全無法**理解**。

Wesley： Pass them over, give us a look!

衛斯理： 傳過來讓我們看看吧！

*** Dave hands the two post-it notes over to Sarah and Wesley***
*** 戴夫將兩張便條遞給莎拉和衛斯理 ***

Post-it note 1:

Dave

Popped out to grab supplies

Back in **a jiffy.**

Katie

便條一：

戴夫

我**出門**拿些補給品

馬上回來。

凱特。

Post-it note 2:

FYI

Gonna try to pick up Krispy Kreme's limited edition **flavs** for the team!

YOLO

K

便條二：

通知你一下

正要去幫大夥兒買些 Krispy Kreme 的限量**口味**甜甜圈。

「**人生苦短，及時行樂**」

凱特。

Sarah： It's from Katie; she's gone to get supplies and hopes to get doughnuts too.

莎拉： 是凱特寫的，她要去買些生活用品，也希望能順便買些甜甜圈。

Wesley： And she said she won't be long.

衛斯理： 她說她不會太久。

Dave： Thanks, I hope she gets the doughnuts. I've been **eyeing up those bad boys** for a few days now.

戴夫： 謝謝，真希望她能買到甜甜圈，我**垂涎**它們好幾天了。

Sarah： **Fingers crossed!**

莎拉： **只能祈求好運囉！**

商英譯起來

wrap my head around

"wrap one's head around" 理解某件困難的事。

post-it note

便利貼，就是我們常見的各種顏色四方型的便條紙。

popped out

"pop out" 出門一下，通常是很快就會回來。

a jiffy

一會兒。

FYI

這是縮寫，"for your information"，提供給您的資訊，這個資料也可以拿來參考並且當作文件的內容。這邊還有另外一個很相似，大家容易搞混的 FYR，"for your reference" 是供您參考的意思，就是信件裡附的資料，只是僅供參考用，所以不一定跟當下的事件有關聯，也不建議拿來當之後編輯文件的內容。

gonna

是 going to (do sth) 的縮寫，表示準備要去做點什麼事。

*sth

=something。

flavs

口味，= flavors，是口語化的縮寫。

YOLO

這是四個字的縮寫，"you only live once"。這是 2013 年，寂寞孤島樂團（The Lonely Island）和魔力紅（Maroon 5）的主唱 Adam Levine 合作的一首歌曲。代表人生就活這麼一次，要大家踏出舒適圈，即時行樂，不害怕的去追逐夢想，不枉此生。

eyeing up those bad boys

"eye up" 很有興趣地盯著……。

fingers crossed

祈禱好運的降臨。將兩隻手的食指和中指交叉，是祈求幸運的意思，"I will keep my fingers crossed for you." 是我會幫你祈禱的意思。

另外有趣的是，如果你發現有個人在面對別人講話時，在身後偷偷將一隻手的食指和中指交叉，那表示他其實是在說謊，說違心之論。

Leave a note
留便條

Dave is trying out some short post-it notes of his own. He has left one on Dean's and Howard's desks describing some recent situations.

戴夫正嘗試利用便利貼溝通，他在迪恩和浩爾的桌上各留一張便條，敘述最近的狀況。

Post-it note 1:

Dean

On cloud 9, let's do beers after work!

O'Brien's at 7.30

I'll fill u in

Dave

便條一：

迪恩

真是爽翻了！下班後去喝一杯吧！

晚上七點半 O'Brien 酒吧見！

到時再跟你說發生什麼事。

戴夫

Post-it note 2:

Howard,

We gotta **weather this storm**

The Regency case **ship has sailed**

Let's not **jump on the bandwagon** just yet,

There're **clouds on the horizon** with **Brexit**

Let's **wait for them to pass**

Meet me in meeting room 7 tomorrow at 8am

Before **the troops** arrive

Dave

便條二：

浩爾

我們得先**挺過這場風波**，

我們**已經錯過** Regency 公司這個案子了，

先別**冒然跟進**

英國脫歐後可能會有許多麻煩。

暫且**靜觀其變**，

明早 8 點在七號會議室見，

在其他**同仁**進辦公室前。

戴夫

商英譯起來

on cloud 9

九霄雲端，樂歪了，欣喜若狂。世界網球名將費德勒 （Roger Federer）在 2017 年澳洲網球公開賽抱走冠軍杯之後約一個月說："I do feel like I'm on cloud 9 still."，表示他非常樂不可支，飄飄然的。

let's do beers

喝酒吧！do 有跟別人一起參與某項活動的意思，如："do a movie"、"do dinner"。

I'll fill you in

我會告知你沒聽到的資訊。"fill sb in"有提供某人消息（漏聽的、錯過的消息）。也可以說 "I'll notify you of further update."，不過後者較正式。

weather this storm

走過風暴；度過難關。

ship has sailed

已錯失良機。

jump on the bandwagon

順勢，一窩蜂跟進。

there're clouds on the horizon

"a cloud on the horizon" 可能到來的後續的麻煩、擔憂。

Brexit

這是一個新造的字，英國（Britain）和撤出（exit）兩個字的合併，就是 Brexit，即代表了「英國脫歐」這件眾所皆知的大事。

wait for them to pass

別著急，等待風波過去。

the troops

部隊，軍隊。在文中指一起工作的同事夥伴們。

Receiving a job rejection email

收到一封工作應徵拒絕電郵

Wesley had decided on a career change and applied for a new **social media influencer position** at a startup company when he received this rejection email.

衛斯理已決定轉換工作跑道，並投履歷到一間新創公司，應徵**社群媒體意見領袖行銷一職**，之後收到這封婉拒信。

Subject: Final Decision Regarding Interview Process

主旨：面試結果

Dear Wesley,

親愛的衛斯理先生：

Thank you very much for taking the time to interview with us for the Social Media Influencer and Marketing position. We

appreciate your interest in the company.

感謝您面試本公司社群媒體意見領袖行銷一職,本公司對於您的熱忱深表感激。

We regret to inform you that you have not been selected for this stage of the application process. We have selected a candidate whom we believe most closely matches the job description of the position **outlined**.

我們很遺憾地通知您,在此一階段您未獲錄取。我們已選出一位與本公司職缺**敘述要求**相符的候選人。

Nonetheless, we will **keep your CV on file should any further positions become available** in the future. **We do not discourage you** from applying for future positions with our company. We are an **equal opportunity employer**.

儘管如此，我們會**將您的履歷建檔**，**待未來有新職缺時**會再與您連絡。**我們歡迎**您再次應徵。本公司對每位申請人**一視同仁**。

We wish you the best of luck in all your **future endeavours.**

祝您未來**一切順利**。

Again, thank you for your time.

Sincerely,

Sally Liu

Hiring Manager

H.R. team.

再次感謝您撥冗閱讀

你誠摯的

人資部主管　劉莎莉

ABC 商英譯起來

social media influencer

社群媒體意見領袖行銷一職。

意見領袖又稱 KOL (Key Opinion Leader)；越來越多消費者仰賴社群媒體購物，包括彩妝，服飾，科技，等甚至家用品，大家都會上網先搜尋評價，透過這樣的意見領袖的粉絲群，得以創造強大的品牌形象。

we regret to inform you

我們非常遺憾的通知您 (通常是某個決定)。

outline

略述；簡單介紹。

nonetheless

然而，儘管如此。有點類似 however 的用法。

keep your CV on file

"keep...on file"，「將⋯⋯建檔」。

should... become available

should 用在這指「萬一⋯⋯的話」或「如果⋯⋯的話」 =" if...becomes available"、 if...should become available"。

we do not discourage you

not 和 discourage（不鼓勵）都是負面的詞彙，但這裡變成了一種負負得正的概念，也就是，我們依然鼓勵你 (去做某件事)。

equal opportunity

機會均等。

future endeavours

為了未來而做的努力，endeavour 與 effort 同意。（endeavour 是英式
的拼法，美式拼法為 endeavor）。

Responding to a job rejection letter
回一封工作拒絕信

Wesley has decided to write a thank you email **following** his rejection email he received. He has decided to put his career change **on the back burner** for now and do some **upskilling**.

衛斯理收到拒絕信後，打算**回覆**一封感謝信。他決定**暫緩**換工作的事情，先學一些**新技能**。

Subject: Thank you note following application for position

主旨：求職感謝信

- -

Dear Ms. Liu,

親愛的劉小姐：

Thank you for taking the time to interview me and show me around the office **amid your tight schedule**. I sincerely enjoyed

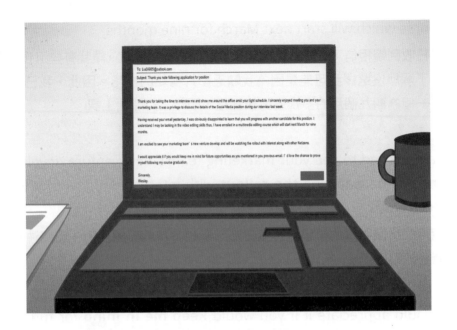

meeting you and your marketing team. It was a privilege to discuss the details of the Social Media position during our interview last week.

感謝您在**百忙之中**抽空與我面談，並帶我參觀辦公室。很高興能跟您及您帶領的行銷團隊見面。上週的面談能與您討論社群媒體一職的細節，實屬我的榮幸。

Having received your email yesterday, I was obviously disappointed to learn that you will progress with another candidate for this position. I understand I may **be lacking in** the video editing skills; **thus**, I have **enrolled in** a multimedia editing course which will start next March for nine months.

昨日收到婉拒信，知道您會找另一位應徵者繼續面試，讓我有些沮喪。我了解您沒選擇我可能是因為我**缺乏**影片剪輯的技巧。**因此**，我已**報名**一個為期九個月的多媒體剪輯課程，明年三月開始上課。

I am excited to see your marketing team's new venture develop and will be watching **the rollout** with interest along with other **Netizens.**

期待您行銷團隊的業績能蒸蒸日上，我也會持續與**網民們**一起關注**新產品的推出**。

I would appreciate it if you would **keep me in mind** for future opportunities as you mentioned in you previous email. I'd love the chance to prove myself following my course graduation.

承您先前提到的，未來如有任何工作機會，您能**想到我**的話，我會非常感激。

我非常樂意在剪輯課程結束後向您證明我的能力。

Sincerely,

Wesley.

謹啟

衛斯理

商英譯起來

following

在……之後沒多久，相當於 after。

on the back burner

(尤指因不緊急或不重要而) 暫時擱置一旁，教人要分辨輕重緩急。

upskilling

upskill，學習新技能；upskilling 是「學習新技能的過程」。

amid your tight schedule

百忙之中。也可說 "amid your busy schedule"。

be lacking in...

「缺乏……」，「在……不足」。

thus

因此。英文的句子講究因果與邏輯，thus 加入逗號，有語氣停頓的加強效果，意思相當於 therefore。

enrolled in

"enrol in" 報名或註冊（某學校 / 課程）。也有人用 "sign up for"。

the rollout

首次推出（產品或服務）。

Netizens

網友們，也是我們俗稱的鄉民。

keep me in mind

記得我，"keep ...in mind" 是「記得……」的意思。

Write a "Dear host family letter"

寫一封給寄宿家庭的信

Dave is writing a sample email for his intern who plans to visit Ireland to study English. The intern would like help writing the email so that he can send it to his **host family** before he arrives in the **Emerald Isle**.

戴夫正在為他的實習生寫一封電郵範本,該生計畫前往愛爾蘭學英語。他需要人幫忙寫電郵,在去**愛爾蘭島**前寄給他的**寄宿家庭**。

Subject: Greeting introduction from a student of IDC Language Centre

主旨:來自 IDC 學生的問候信

Dear Ms. Doherty,

親愛的多爾蒂女士:

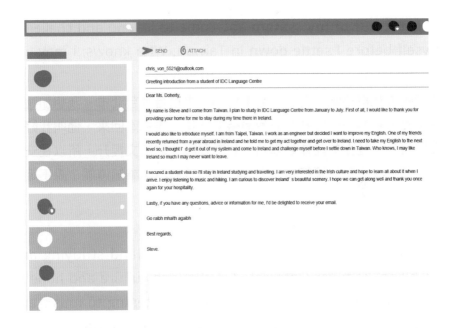

To: chris_von_5521@outlook.com

Greeting introduction from a student of IDC Language Centre

Dear Ms. Doherty,

My name is Steve and I come from Taiwan. I plan to study in IDC Language Centre from January to July. First of all, I would like to thank you for providing your home for me to stay during my time there in Ireland.

I would also like to introduce myself. I am from Taipei, Taiwan. I work as an engineer but decided I want to improve my English. One of my friends recently returned from a year abroad in Ireland and he told me to get my act together and get over to Ireland. I need to take my English to the next level so, I thought I'd get it out of my system and come to Ireland and challenge myself before I settle down in Taiwan. Who knows, I may like Ireland so much I may never want to leave.

I secured a student visa so I'll stay in Ireland studying and travelling. I am very interested in the Irish culture and hope to learn all about it when I arrive. I enjoy listening to music and hiking. I am curious to discover Ireland's beautiful scenery. I hope we can get along well and thank you once again for your hospitality.

Lastly, if you have any questions, advice or information for me, I'd be delighted to receive your email.

Go raibh mhaith agaibh

Best regards,

Steve.

My name is Steve and I come from Taiwan. I plan to study in IDC Language Centre from January to July. First of all, I would like to thank you for providing your home for me to stay during my time there in Ireland.

我是來自台灣的史帝夫。我一月到七月會在愛爾蘭的 IDC 語言中心就讀。首先，我想謝謝您，提供您的家當作我在愛爾蘭的住所。

I would also like to introduce myself. I am from Taipei, Taiwan. I work as an engineer but decided I want to improve my English. One of my friends recently returned from a year abroad in Ireland and he told me **to get my act together** and get over to Ireland. I need to take my English to the next level so, I thought

I'd **get it out of my system** and come to Ireland and challenge myself before I settle down in Taiwan. Who knows, I may like Ireland so much I may never want to leave.

介紹一下我自己吧。我是一名工程師,來自台灣台北市。我想加強我的英文,我的一位好友在愛爾蘭待了一年,最近剛回來,他叫我**好好安排自己**,並立刻前往愛爾蘭。我需要讓我的英文提升,所以在安定成家前,我決定**付諸行動**,來愛爾蘭挑戰自己。誰知道呢?說不定我會愛上這裡,不想回家呢!

I **secured** a student visa so I'll stay in Ireland studying and travelling. I am very interested in the Irish culture and hope to learn all about it when I arrive. I enjoy listening to music and hiking. I am curious to discover Ireland's beautiful scenery. I hope we can get along well and thank you once again for your **hospitality**.

我已**拿**到學生簽證,接下來會在愛爾蘭讀書、旅行。我對愛爾蘭文化非常有興趣,希望在這段時間能對愛爾蘭有多一點認識。我喜愛聽音樂及健行,渴望發掘愛爾蘭的美景。希望我們能相處愉快,再次感謝您的**照顧**。

Lastly, if you have any questions, advice or information for me, **I'd be delighted to** receive your email.

Go raibh mhaith agaibh

最後,如您有任何疑問、建議或資訊要提供給我,**歡迎**隨時來信。

非常感謝!

Best regards,

Steve.

祝好

史帝夫

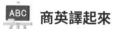 **商英譯起來**

host family
寄宿家庭。

Emerald Isle
愛爾蘭島。也有人稱之為翡翠島或是綠寶石島。

get my act together
好好安排自己（讓自己做事有效率）；振作起來。

get it out of my system
付諸行動（做自己一直想做卻沒做的事）；發洩（負面的情緒或慾望）。

secured
secure，獲得；設法得到，意思想當於 obtain。

go raibh mhaith agaibh
愛爾蘭文的「謝謝」，與 "thank you" 同意。

hospitality
友好；好客；款待

I'd be delighted to...
"I'd be pleased to..."，「我很高興能……」。

Quotation and Budgets
報價與預算

Dean is emailing Frank, a potential **vendor** who had previously given a **quotation** which was over budget. Dean has decided to respond and inform him about this information.

迪恩正在寫郵件給一位潛在**供應商**法蘭克，該廠先前給出的**報價**超過公司預算。迪恩決定寫信告知他這項資訊。

Subject: Decision on RSD case
主旨：RSD 之定案

Dear Frank,
親愛的法蘭克：

I appreciate you providing a current quotation which shows your interest in **collaborating** with us for our upcoming project.

Unfortunately, we will not have an opportunity to work together on this case due to our **tight** budget guidelines which have been **passed down to** me by senior management. I hope we will have another chance to cooperate in the future.

感謝您目前針對我們未來的企劃所提供的報價，並表示您有**合作的意願**。然而，我**剛收到**公司主管給我的預算**縮減**政策，因此我們無法一起合作這項專案了，希望未來我們能再有機會共事。

Sincere regards,

Dean

敬祝順心

迪恩

Frank responds with an email asking the exact price difference and if there are any other reasons as to why they cannot work together on the case.

*** 法蘭克回覆迪恩的信件，他想知道確切價差，
以及是否有其他理由導致他們無法合作 ***

Good afternoon Dean,

午安，迪恩：

It is indeed a shame to hear this news. For our records, could you please advise on what **grounds** we were unsuccessful and what was the exact price difference?

很遺憾收到這個消息。為方便記錄，可以請您告知我確切價差以及不能合作的原因嗎？

Regards,

Frank.

祝好

法蘭克

商英譯起來

vendor

賣方；供應商；小販。

quotation

估價單。一般會涵蓋貨品描述、數量、交貨日期、地點、聯絡人、單價，及是否可有替代品等詳細資訊。

collaborating

collaborate，合作。與 cooperate 意思相近。collaborate 屬於共同合作完成某事。cooperate 則強調另一方的某些協助。

tight

（時間、錢）緊的，拮据的。

passed down to

"pass down to" 是「（資訊或是傳統）傳下來」的意思。

Sincere regards

敬祝順心。通常為信件尾端禮貌的用語。也有人寫做，"Kind regards"、"Yours sincerely" 或是 "Your truly"。

ground

ground 除了地上這個意思以外，也可當「依據、原因」，也可說「根據什麼理由」，"on what grounds"。

Price Negotiation
講價

Following on the previous unit's topic; Dean has decided to use another vendor for this project unless Frank can reduce his quote. Dean is using another vendor's cheaper quote **as leverage** to try to get Frank to reduce his price. Dean knows and understands that Frank's company is a better company to use based on their quality and efficiency.

在上一個單元中，除非法蘭克降低報價，否則迪恩將找其他供應商合作。迪恩利用其他報價更便宜的廠商**當作籌碼**，試圖壓低法蘭克的價格。迪恩心裡明白，就效率和品質來看，法蘭克的公司更勝一籌。

Subject: Final Decision on RSD Case
主旨：關於 RSD 案子的最終決定

Good morning Frank,
早安，法蘭克：

Following our previous email, we have decided **to press forward** with our project using another vendor as their quotation was within our management's budget plan. I am sure you can appreciate this.

上封信我們決定與另一個廠商**繼續進行**這項專案，因為他的報價更符合我們的預算，相信您能理解。

For your reference, the difference in the quotation was **quite substantial** and I doubt you could match their figure. **Should you wish to collaborate with us** on this project, you would have to reduce your initial quote by at least 12%.

僅提供您參考，報價的價差**甚巨**，我不確定您的價格能否降到與他們一樣的價格。**如果您希望跟我們合作**，您最初的報價必須降低至少 12%。

If this is something you could offer us **I would appreciate a response by the end of business today** as we aim to stick to our **project management timeline**. If I don't hear from you I will assume you are unable to match our budget guidelines.

如果您可以提供我們較低的價格，請在今天下班前給我們回覆，以利我們**維持專案的進度**。如果今天未收到您的回覆，我將視為您無法提供降價。

I look forward to your prompt response,
期待收到您的即時回覆！

Regards,
Dean.
祝好
迪恩

商英譯起來

leverage

籌碼，影響。這是一個極具戰略意義的字眼，華爾街常用 "maximum leverage" 表示充分利用到極致。比如身上有一萬塊錢，就去借一百萬，把房屋證券化，以衍生出保險等其他產品。

to press forward

繼續進行。

quite substantial

相當可觀。

should you wish to collaborate with...

若您希望合作 (某件案子)，should 相當於 if。

if it's something you could offer

offer 是「提供」，這裡的意思為 (上述提到的) 若是您可以為我方提供 (產品，資料等)。

I would appreciate a response by the end of business today

"business day" 是上班日的意思，"by the end of business day"，在今日的上班時間結束前，也就是下班前希望能收到回覆的意思。

project management timeline

專案執行時間表，希望掌握進度的意思。

I look forward to your prompt response

很期待能收到您即時的回覆。"Look forward to" 很常用在信的結尾，如 "I look forward to seeing you soon."，很期待很快能見到你。

Erros and Mistakes
失誤和錯誤

Dave has come to Howard for some help on how to understand an email he is having trouble with. The email is from a supplier from Croatia. There are many mistakes and errors within the email and Dave hopes Howard can help him correct it. Howard has underlined the main mistakes and errors to avoid.

戴夫請浩爾幫忙看一封讓他一頭霧水的電郵。電郵是來自克羅埃西亞的供應商。信上有許多失誤和錯誤，戴夫希望浩爾能幫忙修正。浩爾將主要的錯誤畫線。

Subject: Update on our new range of products

熟識友人才使用 hey 加上名字打招呼，不帶姓氏。
一般交情使用 hello 或 hi。最禮貌客氣則使用 "Dear Mr./Ms./Mrs." 加上姓氏。

Hey Madam David,

性別錯誤。David 顯然是男性，而不是女士 madam。

少了動詞。我的名字是 my name is。

少了動詞和定冠詞。我是新任 I am the new。

My name Costa I new supply consultant for our company in Dubrovnik. We hope collaboration can happen next terms and we supplies many ranges for you needs.

語意不明。不如略去，或指明預計合作時間。

我們提供許多範圍，語意不明，可整理成形容詞和名詞結構 "our wide range of supplies" 或者 "we offer a wide selection of supplies"。

應為所有格 your。

應是指「有機會」，應改為 "I hope we can have this opportunity to..."。

新範圍，意味不明。

更安全應寫 safer。

New ranges offer special technology and more safe aspects to you offices spaces. Hope we can sometimes provide products when you needs them anytime can no problem for our company. We give you cheap price and top quality handmade Croatia.

提供⋯⋯給您的辦公室或公司，寫 "to your office" 即可。

意味不明。

應為過去式 gave。

應為過去式 "did you"。

Yesterday, I give you new catalogue. Do you receive new catalogue. Inside have cheap price but if you have big number bulk order please sir contact to me to help more cheap for you to connect email anytime for you be our service and happy to help.

請見正確建議版及中文翻譯。

Speak soons we hear from you response asap Sir David

希望盡快得到您的回覆，應該為
"We hope to hear from you as soon as possible"。

Many thanks,

Costa

正確建議版

Subject: Update on our new range of products
主旨：新一期產品更新。

Good morning David,
早安，大衛。

My name is Costa and I am the new supply chain manager based in Dubrovnik. We are happy to supply you to satisfy all your business needs.

我是杜布羅夫尼克供應鏈的新任主管，哥斯達。很榮幸能擔任您的供應商，我們會竭誠滿足您的商業需求。

We currently have a new range of products which we feel will **add to** your office environment and atmosphere. Please see our catalogue attached **for your consideration**. All our products are handmade and **adhere to** international standards.

我們目前擁有一系列的新產品，我們認為這些產品將為您的辦公環境及氛圍**增添**新氣息。請見附件目錄**以供參考**，我們的產品皆是手工製造，且**符合**國際標準。

Please let me know if you have any trouble viewing the catalogue. The prices **quoted** in the catalogue can be **negotiated should you wish to buy in bulk or large orders.** If you have any requests or queries relating to our products and lead delivery time please get in touch.

如果對目錄有任何問題，請與我們聯繫。

若您有意要大量批發，**目錄上的價格**均可再議。如果您對產品或**提前期／交貨期**有任何要求或疑問，請隨時與我們保持聯繫。

Best wishes,

Costa.

祝好

哥斯達

ABC 商英譯起來

add to...

增添……氣息 / 感覺。

for your consideration

供您參考。

adhere to

遵守。

quoted

quote（v.）報價。"the prices quoted in the catalogue"目錄中所報的價格。

negotiated

negotiate（v.）談判；協商。

lead/ delivery time

提前期 / 交貨期。"lead time"是指從採購方開始下單訂購到供應商交貨所間隔的時間。"delivery time"是指賣方將貨物裝上運往目的地的運輸工具或交付承運人的日期。

A complaint email
客訴信

Wesley has just come back from a business trip in Melbourne, Australia but he wasn't happy with the service and state of the hotel that he stayed in. He has decided to write a complaint email with the hope of receiving some **acceptable compensation** following the unpleasant experience.

衛斯理剛從澳洲墨爾本出差回來，但他對旅館品質及服務相當不滿。於是他決定寫一封客訴信，希望旅館針對這次不愉快的經驗，給出**合理的賠償**。

Subject: FAO Customer services manager
       - My recent stay at your hotel
主旨：急郵！致客服部主管：關於近日下榻貴旅館的事宜。

Dear Customer Services Manager,
致客服部主管：

I recently stayed in your hotel for two nights whilst on a recent business trip. Some colleagues in Sydney had been **raving about** your place for the last few months so I decided to **give it a shot.** However, I was left feeling disappointed following my stay. It wasn't **the best thing since sliced bread** which is what I was led to believe following my colleague's recommendation.

我最近因公出差，在你們旅館住了兩晚。在我登記入住的前幾個月，許多在雪梨的同事都跟我**大力稱讚**你們的旅館，所以我決定**給你們旅館一個機會**，但入住後卻感到頗失望。顯然，這次經驗不如我同事推薦的那麼好。

I arrived on the **specified** check in date and **was greeted by** an unfriendly and quite rude reception staff member at the front desk. Her name was Helen Smith and she didn't make me feel welcome. I had booked a **non-smoking business suite;** however,when I entered my room I noticed that there was a strong smell of smoke.

我在**指定的**入住時間到達，但**接待**我的櫃檯人員卻不太友善、甚至有些沒禮貌。她的名字是海倫‧史密斯，她的態度讓我感覺不受歡迎。我預訂的是**無菸商務套房**，但當我進房後就聞到一股濃濃的菸味。

I complained but there was nothing that could be done as the hotel was fully booked. This was unprofessional and extremely frustrating as I don't smoke and had specifically requested a non-smoking room.

我向工作人員反應了這個狀況，但當天旅館已客滿，所以也不能幫我處理。對一個不吸菸、且已預訂無菸套房的人來說，你們的處理方式極不專業且令人非常失望。

Another thing which was disappointing was there was no iron or ironing board in the room. I **rang down to the reception** and they sent an iron and board up to the room but that didn't work. So, when I called back down again I was told that there were no more left. This made me angry as I needed **fresh shirts** for my business meetings.

另一件令人失望的事是房間裡沒有熨斗及燙衣板。我**打到櫃檯**，他們送來了熨斗和燙衣板，但卻壞了。當我再打給櫃檯時，他們卻說沒有熨斗可提供了。這讓我很生氣,因為我出席會議需要**平整**的襯衫。

Finally, I scheduled a wake-up call for the second morning however; I never got that call which meant I was late for work. Overall, the experience was disappointing and frustrating and I don't think I would recommend the hotel to friends and family. Having listed my complaints I feel a refund would be fair compensation for the distress, work missed and frustration caused. **I would hate to have to** contact **the Ombudsman** with this **complaint** and I would hope for it **to be rectified before any further action is taken.**

最後,我預訂了隔天早上的電話提醒服務,但我卻沒有接到電話,結果我上班遲到。總而言之,這次住宿經驗令我非常失望,我想我也不會推薦這間旅館給親朋好友。列出所有細項後,我認為這次住宿經驗所導致的失望、工作遲到及沮喪,向你們要求退費賠償是合理的。我**不希望**最後我要向**消保官申訴**,希望在我進一步**採取任何行動前**,你們可以**處理好**這件事。

Looking forward to your response,

靜候您的回覆

Regards,

Wesley

祝好

衛斯理

 **商英譯起來**

acceptable compensation

合理的賠償。

FAO

這個是縮寫，"for the attention of"，通常放在郵件的開頭主旨，代表緊急郵件，提示內容很重要必須優先處理。

raving about

"rave about"，讚不絕口，熱烈吹捧。跟 praise 和 compliment 意思相近。

give it a shot

試試看，也可用 "give it a go"。

the best thing since sliced bread

有史以來最棒的事。slice 是單位詞，指「切片的」。美國在 1928 年前販售的麵包是大塊且沒有切片的。後來 Otto Frederick Rohwedder 發明了美國人最愛的切麵包機，此後，只要是說到什麼東西超棒的，就用這句話來形容。

specified

指定的，也可用 appointed 或是 set。

was greeted by

"be greeted by"，被（某人）迎接。

non-smoking business suite

無菸商務套房。

rang down to the reception

rung 是 ring 過去式。 "ring down to the reception" 是打電話到樓下櫃台。

fresh shirts

乾淨沒皺痕的襯衫。

I would hate to have to

沒必要我真的不願意（做某件事）。

the ombudsman

（政府或處理投訴的）申訴專員、消保官。

to be rectified

"rectify"，糾正、改正，也可作 fix。

before any further action is taken

採取更多行動之前。

Week 49
Cover Letter
求職信

Howard has received an email from Mike, who is applying for a job opening at the company. The email was sent to Howard by mistake so he passed it to the HR department.

浩爾收到了麥克要應徵公司職務的求職信，該求職信是誤寄給浩爾的，浩爾收到後轉寄給人資部。

Subject: Marketing Officer Position

主旨：行銷主管一職

Dear Hiring Manager,

致人資部經理：

My name is Mike Chen and I am applying **for the titled position** of Marketing Officer Position at your company. I have over six

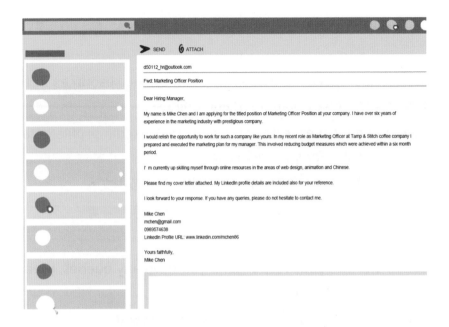

years of experience in the marketing industry with prestigious companies.

我的名字是陳麥克,想應徵貴公司的行銷主管**一職**。我曾在一間業界有名的公司工作,有六年的行銷實務經驗。

I would **relish the opportunity to** work for such a company like yours. In my recent role as Marketing Officer at Tamp & Stitch coffee company I prepared and **executed** the marketing plan for my manager. This involved reducing budget measures which were achieved within a six month period.

我**希望有機會能**為您這樣的優良企業工作。我最後一份在 Tamp & Stitch 咖啡的工作是行銷主管,工作內容為幫主管企劃及**執行**行銷企劃。工作期間，我成功在六個月內幫公司縮減預算。

I'm currently upskilling myself through online resources in the areas of web design, animation and Chinese.

Please find my **cover letter** attached. My LinkedIn profile details are included also for your reference.

目前我正利用網路資源學習網頁設計、動畫製作及中文。

隨信附上我的**求職信**與領英網的詳細個人資料，供您參考。

I look forward to your response. If you have any queries, **please do not hesitate to contact me.**

期待收到您的回覆。如有任何疑問，**請立即與我聯繫**。

Mike Chen

mchen@gmail.com

0989574638

LinkedIn Profile URL: www.linkedin.com/mchen86

Yours faithfully,

Mike Chen

謹啟

陳麥克

商英譯起來

Dear hiring manager

信件的抬頭。也可以寫作 "To whom it may concern" 也就是敬啟者的意思。如果你透過管道得知了人資主管的姓名，也可直接打上姓，若否則可如文中使用 "Dear hiring manager" 也是很恰當的。

for the titled position

職位，其實也就是 "for the job" 的意思。

relish the opportunity

期望能有這樣的機會 （做某件事）。opportunity 和 chance 常會被互換使用，然而它們的意思卻有著些微的不同。chance 是機率，大部分是偶然的機會，經常含有僥倖的意味。opportunity 多指特殊的機會，含有期待、願望的感覺。當 chance 表示可能性的時候，則不能用 opportunity 代替。

executed

execute，「執行（某個計畫）」。manage、"deal with"、"carry out" 也都有相同的意思。

cover letter

求職信，說明為何應徵該工作及簡單自我介紹，可當作履歷的開場白，通常與履歷一同寄給開職缺的公司。

please do not hesitate to contact me

意即請別猶豫，歡迎與我聯絡。

Medical examination results

健康檢查報告

Dave has just received an email from his friend Patrick who is a doctor at the local hospital. Dave recently had a full health examination following some health concerns he experienced.

戴夫剛收到好友派崔克的郵件，派崔克目前在地方醫院擔任醫師。戴夫最近健康有些問題，於是做了全身健康檢查。

Hi Dave,

嗨！戴夫：

Good to see you the last time you came in to have your full health check. I just want to **check in with you**. As your friend, I have **to be frank** with you. The **diagnosis** has come back to me this morning and it's not good. You're **sailing too close to the wind** right now. Your blood results are the most concerning. It appears you have early **onset** of **type I diabetes** and potentially

you could be facing **a stroke** if you do not dramatically change your lifestyle.

很高興在上次的健康檢查中見到你，這封信只是想**確認你的狀況**。身為朋友我必須向你**坦承**，我今早收到**診斷**，結果不是很好，你的**身體狀況不太好**。你的驗血結果令人擔憂，其顯示**第一型糖尿病**正在**發作**。如果你沒有大幅調整作息，有可能會**中風**。

All major diseases such as HIV/AIDS/Hep. A/C and cancers are **conclusively negative**. Blood pressure is higher than normal and your **red blood cell count** is low.

其他重大疾病如人類免疫缺陷病毒、愛滋病、A 和 C 型肝炎以及癌症**皆顯示陰性**。你的血壓高於平均值，**紅血球數量**也偏低。

My next recommendation is for you come back into see me **at some stage** this week. I will have Joan, my secretary **give you a bell** later today to arrange a meeting. **Don't hang about** Dave. **I'll do all in my power to help you.** See you soon.

接下來，我建議你這週**找時間**再來找我檢查。稍後我會請我的秘書瓊**致電**給你，以便安排會面時間。戴夫，別對此**不以為意，我會盡全力幫你**。回頭見。

Cheers,

Pat

派崔克　上

商英譯起來

check in with you
（通過打電話，拜訪等確認或報告某人是否無恙）與……取得聯繫；查看。

to be frank
坦承告知。與 "to be honest" 用法相同。

diagnosis
（醫療相關的）診斷。

are sailing too close to the wind
"sail too close to the wind"，冒風險；在危險邊緣。

type 1 diabetes
第一型糖尿病，也稱做「青少年糖尿病」或是「胰島素依賴型糖尿病」，無法預防，一般於兒童或是青壯年開始發病。

onset
（指不愉快的事情、疾病）的開始，發作。

stroke
中風。

conclusively negative
結論皆為陰性（醫療診斷相關）。如果檢查結果是 positive（陽性），就表示篩檢顯示生病了！

red blood cell count

紅血球計數，也就是紅血球的數量的意思。count 在這裡為名詞是總數的意思。

at some stage

某些時候，意思等同"at some time"。

give you a bell

致電。也可使用"give you a call"。

don't hang about

別置之不理，表示希望自己或對方能做點有助於情況的事。

I'll do all in my power to help you

我會盡全力幫助你的。也可寫作"I'll do my best to help you"。

Week 51

An idiom overload email
充滿俚語的電郵

Dave has received an email from one of his coworkers from Ireland which is full of idioms and phrases that he doesn't understand. He has asked Dean to help him figure out what Stephen wants him to do.

戴夫收到一位愛爾蘭同事寄來的電子郵件，信件內滿滿都是他不懂的片語和慣用語。於是戴夫向迪恩請教史蒂芬在信中究竟要他做什麼。

Subject: **Touch base**
主旨：**狀況告知**

Hi Dave,
戴夫你好，

I've been onto Karl in marketing and he thinks it's a **no-brainer** that we move forward with the ApexVivo case. I've gotten **the**

green light from Bill, the head of supply chain. I was **at sixes and sevens** until I spoke to Bill and it's just like **breaking the seal**. So, go ahead and look for that **loophole** we spoke about last week.

我和行銷部的卡爾聊過,他認為我們**不用多想**,可以繼續 ApexVivo 的案子,我也已**徵得**供應鏈主管比爾的**同意**。在和比爾談之前,我內心一直**七上八下**,聊完之後總算**豁然開朗**,所以就繼續尋找上周談到的那**漏洞**吧。

Going forward, we need to let that information **trickle down** to others in the department. Don't worry about that previous link attached, it's **clickbait** nonsense. Regarding the new case in

Geneva, it's **a blessing in disguise** that they rejected our initial offer.

接著，我們得讓部門的其他人**慢慢**知道這資訊。無須理會之前附上的連結，那些都是毫無意義的**釣魚網站**。另外，關於日內瓦的新案子，他們拒絕了我們當初的提議，可說是**因禍得福**。

My advice is to **keep a low profile** for the next few weeks until this entire circus **blows over**.

我個人建議，在接下來的幾周**保持低調**，直到這整場鬧劇**逐漸平息**。

Keep me posted,
Stephen
保持聯絡
史蒂芬 敬上

ABC 商英譯起來

touch base
與（某人）取得聯繫；聊聊，談談。

no brainer
根本不須加以思考，就知道的決定或答案。

the green light
批准。好比開車過路口，看到綠燈可以通行不用擔心會被罰款，所以這句也有給予便利，放行的意思。

at sixes and sevens
亂七八糟，一團亂。

breaking the seal
原意為打開封口，瓶蓋等。在這裡有解開疑慮，豁然開朗的意思。

loophole
事件的漏洞，破綻。

going forward
接下來。後面通常接要講的或是即將發生的事情，也可與 next 交替使用。

trickle down
涓滴效應，也可翻譯做滲漏效應或是滴漏效應。表示從上司到下屬，循序漸進，慢慢一點一點滲透。

clickbait

釣魚連結。click 是滑鼠按下去「按」的動作，bait 是誘餌，加起來表示，看起來很有趣或聳動的新聞標題，吸引讀者點閱，以點閱率來創造營收，也有很多是誘騙詐騙的網站。

a blessing in disguise

因禍得福。成語中的「塞翁失馬，焉知非福」也可以用這句話來表示。

keep a low profile

保持低調。"high profile" 則為反義詞，高調。

blows over

"blow over" 意指 (爭論或風波) 逐漸平息。

Scam email
詐騙電郵

Dean has received an email from the bank and they have asked him to confirm some details. He checks with Wesley to confirm that the email is **legitimate**. He fears it may be a scam.

迪恩收到一封銀行寄來的電子郵件，對方要求他確認一些細節。迪恩找衛斯理來確認該信是否**正常**。他擔心可能是詐騙信件。

Dean： Wesley, could you come have a look at this?

迪恩： 衛斯理，你可以來看一下這個嗎？

Wesley： Sure, what is it?

衛斯理： 好啊，怎麼了？

Dean： I got an email from my bank this morning. However, I can't tell if it is **a scam** or not. Here it is:

迪恩： 我今早從銀行那邊收到一封電郵，不過我不確定是不是**詐騙信**，就是這封：

From: CEO@softbank237.com

Subject: Security threat of your savings account. URGENT!

主旨：緊急！帳戶的安全威脅。

Dear **Account Holder**,

親愛的**帳戶持有人**您好：

We wish to inform you that there has been **a malicious attack** on your savings account made on **12/04**. In order to secure the contents of your account we require you to confirm your 4 digit pin number. Please click our company registered link below to enter your pin number and full name and account number. We will be sure to protect and secure your funds immediately. Please do this ASAP as you are a valued member of our company.

我們想通知您，您的儲蓄戶頭在 **4 月 12 日遭到惡意攻擊**。為確保您的帳號安全，我們需要向您確認您的 4 位密碼。請點擊下方本公司的註冊連結，輸入您的密碼、全名和帳號。我們將立即確保您的資金安全。請盡快完成以上步驟，我們希望保障重要的客戶。

Yours,

John Smith,

CEO, Softbank.

Soft 銀行總裁約翰‧史密斯 敬上

Wesley： That's a complete scam, man. My best advice to you is to call your bank and change your email address. Perhaps set up **encryption software** on your computer if you can. Do you have anti-virus software **in place**?

衛斯理： 老兄這一看就是詐騙啊，我建議你最好打電話給你的銀行，然後改一下你的電郵地址。可以的話，裝個**加密軟體**吧，你**該裝**的防毒有裝嗎？

Dean： Not yet, but I **won't hang about**.

迪恩： 還沒，不過我**這就去用**。

商英譯起來

legitimate
正當的，合法的。

scam
騙局，詐欺，詐騙。fraud 則為罪名，詐騙罪。而詐欺者為 scammer 或是 fraudster。

threat
威脅。

account holder
帳戶持有人。

a malicious attack
惡意攻擊，對電腦系統或個人資訊進行破壞或竊取。malicious 也可寫作 vicious，同樣都是惡毒的意思。

12/04
日期的表達可能有兩種：12/4 ＝四月十二日（歐制）；12/4 ＝十二月四日（美制）。

encryption software
（資料）加密軟體。

in place
準備妥當。

hang about
置之不理。

| 創譯兄弟商英職人養成術 - 52 週英文質感優雅升級

Linking English
創譯兄弟商英職人養成術：52週英文質感優雅升級

2019年11月初版   定價：新臺幣480元
有著作權・翻印必究
Printed in Taiwan.

著　　　者	許皓 Wesley	
	浩爾 Howard	
	Dean Brownless	
叢書主編	李　　　芃	
翻譯協力	楊　巖　傑	
	何　孟　倫	
校　　　對	劉　彥　珈	
	劉　詠　庭	
插　　　畫	Erique Chong	
整體設計	Anzo Design Co.	
編輯主任	陳　逸　華	

出　版　者	聯經出版事業股份有限公司	總編輯	胡　金　倫
地　　　址	新北市汐止區大同路一段369號1樓	總經理	陳　芝　宇
編輯部地址	新北市汐止區大同路一段369號1樓	社　長	羅　國　俊
叢書編輯電話	(02)86925588轉5317	發行人	林　載　爵
台北聯經書房	台北市新生南路三段94號		
電　　　話	(02)23620308		
台中分公司	台中市北區崇德路一段198號		
暨門市電話	(04)22312023		
台中電子信箱	e-mail：linking2@ms42.hinet.net		
郵政劃撥帳戶第0100559-3號			
郵撥電話	(02)23620308		
印　刷　者	文聯彩色製版印刷有限公司		
總　經　銷	聯合發行股份有限公司		
發　行　所	新北市新店區寶橋路235巷6弄6號2樓		
電　　　話	(02)29178022		

行政院新聞局出版事業登記證局版臺業字第0130號

本書如有缺頁，破損，倒裝請寄回台北聯經書房更換。　　ISBN　978-957-08-5417-6 (平裝)
電子信箱：linking@udngroup.com

國家圖書館出版品預行編目資料

創譯兄弟商英職人養成術：52週英文質感優雅升級/
浩爾、許皓、Dean Brownless著 . 初版 . 新北市 . 聯經 . 2019年11月 .
320面 . 14.8×21公分（Linking English）
ISBN 978-957-08-5417-6（平裝）

1.商業英文 2.讀本

805.18 108019096